Homecoming Homicides

by

Marilyn Baron

A Psychic Crystal Mystery
Book Two

Homecoming Homicides

Cover Art by *Debbie Taylor*

The Wild Rose Press, Inc.
PO Box 708
Adams Basin, NY 14410-0708
Visit us at www.thewildrosepress.com

Publishing History
First Crimson Rose Edition, 2014
Print ISBN 978-1-62830-196-0
Digital ISBN 978-1-62830-197-7

A Psychic Crystal Mystery, Book Two
Published in the United States of America

Praise for Marilyn Baron

Winner of the Georgia Romance Writers
Unpublished Maggie Award for Excellence in 2012
in the Paranormal/Fantasy Romance category
First Place Winner in the Suspense Romance Category
of the 2010 Ignite the Flame contest
sponsored by the Central Ohio Fiction Writers chapter
of Romance Writers of America
Finalist in the Georgia Romance Writers
Unpublished Maggie Award for Excellence in 2005
in the Single Title Category

"Baron offers a bit of everything in this superb novel. There's humor, infidelity, murder, mayhem, and a neatly drawn conclusion."

~RT Book Reviews (4.5 Stars)

"I just finished reading *UNDER THE MOON GATE* and really enjoyed it. I was fascinated by the intertwining of the characters in the stories from the 1700s to present day and I especially enjoyed the segment that took place during WWII. Great writing. Marilyn did a great job of bringing Bermuda during the WWII era to life in this book."

~PJ Ausdenmore, The Romance Dish

"[*UNDER THE MOON GATE*] is a surefire blockbuster...a treasure trove of mystery and intrigue. It sparkles with romance.... I couldn't recommend it more."

~Andrew Kirby

"An enjoyable read from start to finish...family, friends, enemies, intrigue and suspense...sadness, laughter, romance and ultimately love."

~Romance Junkies (4 Blue Ribbons)

"Flippy, I mean Philippa, uh, Miss Tannenbaum, there's an Officer Luke Slaughter from the Graysville Police Department here to see you."

Despite her practiced calm, carefully cultivated from her beauty queen days, Flippy's stomach shuddered as a tremor rumbled through her body. The seismic shift seized her fragile heart. She had never expected to see Luke Slaughter again, much less this soon, fully clothed, and certainly not under these circumstances.

"Send him in, Misty."

Had she managed to keep the vibrating waves of tension from her voice? Just barely. She squeezed her eyes shut, remembering the last time she'd seen Luke Slaughter, bare and naked, sleeping beside her in her dump of an apartment. Actually, he'd had her in an unconscious octopus hold, hands everywhere, possessively clutching her body like so many tentacles, cutting off her circulation so she could barely breathe. At least it felt like she was suffocating. Had it only been a week ago? Could she face him here after what they'd done (what hadn't they done?), and after how shabbily she'd treated him when the night was over? Despite the nauseated feeling in her stomach, the answer was "yes," but it wouldn't be fun.

Dedication

Homecoming Homicides is dedicated to my daughter,
Amanda,
who was a homecoming contestant at her university
in a small North Florida town.
When I attended the pageant, a seemingly innocent
"boy-man" approached each girl to get her autograph
on his pageant booklet.
That sparked my imagination and was the inspiration
for this story.

Prologue

Rodney Willis inhaled the aroma of fresh blood. In his opinion, nothing else even came close to the scent of suffering. The blood was slick and sticky and velvety, and he was practically swimming in it. He'd nearly slipped on the floor this morning while he was in full clean-up mode, getting ready for the new contestant. He needed to buy some combat boots.

The candidate on the table had been a real trooper. He had to give her credit. She'd performed superbly, even exceeded his expectations, although she was rather noisy. He'd had to muffle her screams. The bitch had bitten him, had probably given him rabies, if that was possible. He'd have to research that on the Internet. Not exactly a candidate for Miss Congeniality. He was finally forced to drug the little vixen, and after that it wasn't nearly as much fun.

When she'd come around again, she complained of the cold. He had to keep the temperature of his workshop near freezing, so he'd obligingly covered her with a blanket and softly soothed her with meaningless prattle while he continued his work. She was pathetically grateful, probably holding out hope that he wouldn't kill her if he was considerate enough to cover her. It suited him to kill her with kindness for the time being. It made it easier for him in the end. He nearly swooned as he remembered the touch of his hand on her naked breast, the feel of her pulsating heartbeat as it tripped like a frightened rabbit and then slowed in resignation, finally sliding into defeat as it stopped altogether when the blood had drained from her body.

And speaking of hearts, he was going to have to have a long overdue heart-to-heart with his big brother, Donny. Last night had been too close for comfort. The screams and moans and tiresome begging sounds coming out of his workshop had drawn the idiot to the door, and he'd had to do some fancy footwork to get him to go away. Donny knew the workshop was off limits, and yet he couldn't help poking around. He had been looking for Traci; he wouldn't have wanted to see what was left of her.

Donny was dangerously fixated on that girl. Rodney had allowed him to stay for the contest and watch Traci model Queenie's dresses, but he didn't get to view the aftermath. Someone of Donny's delicate nature would never understand what had to be done. He always wondered where the girls had gone, and he'd always been satisfied when Rodney had said, "They had a previous engagement." But not this time. Not with Traci Farris.

Donny had to be kept in the dark. Rodney needed Donny's help in carrying the bodies, which Rodney would lovingly clean and delicately wrap, like Egyptian mummies. Donny was stronger than an ox. Donny's father had been big and strong, too. Strong enough to beat up on his son anytime the mood hit him, which was often, when he was done using his wife, Queenie, as his personal punching bag, until she killed him with his own shotgun. Rodney's own father had left them a long time ago, left Queenie to raise her two boys alone.

Donny was special, but Queenie always said both her boys were special to her.

Rodney had inherited his mother's slimness and good looks. Everyone said he favored Queenie. And that Rodney took as a supreme compliment. After all, Queenie was a winner.

He looked over at his mother's picture and smiled. "There's no one like you, Queenie. Never was before, never will be again. Only one even comes close."

He'd promised his brother another scavenger hunt tonight, a reverse scavenger hunt. They weren't hunting for anyone. Instead, they were delivering something. Donny wasn't to ask what was in the package. That would ruin the fun. Rodney had picked out the new dump site, and he could hardly wait until it got dark.

He knew the rules of jurisdiction. As long as he continued to dump the bodies on campus, the FBI couldn't get involved unless they were invited in. And the campus police and the city cops—more like the Keystone Kops—were clueless. They had no intention of asking the Feds to their party. In the end, they'd bowed to public pressure. With the notoriety of the case, the outraged parents had demanded it. But as far as he was concerned, even with the FBI intervention, it wasn't an even match. He was already on Contestant Number Six, and they had no idea who he was or when he would strike next or why he was doing what he was doing. At this rate, he'd rack up his goal of thirty girls in no time.

He was rather enjoying this little contest of wits. Of course, now that the FBI was involved, he'd have to be more careful. FBI or no FBI, the campus police and city police were engaged in a pissing contest, and they were so busy getting in each other's way they'd left the field wide open for him. Unfortunately, they had thrown a wrench into his plans when they called in Crystal Ball Kate, that psychic he'd seen all over the news. But she was no match for someone of his skills and abilities. And, just for fun, he might teach her a lesson, too.

Tomorrow, after work, he would go trolling for Contestant Number Seven, and he would save the best—Katherine Crystal—now Katherine Crystal Hale—for last, unless an opportunity to snatch his prize came along earlier. Then he wouldn't be able to resist her. He'd jump right on it. It would be more difficult, considering she was now a consultant for the Graysville Police Department. And that big brute of a husband of hers, Beauregard somebody or other, would be guarding her around the clock.

But he was smarter than they were. And he was an insider, which was his advantage. He'd managed to kill Melinda Crawford right under the nose of that campus cop who had somehow transferred over to the Graysville City police force and was now guarding one of the homecoming contestants. Eventually that cop would let his guard down, and then he would make his move at exactly the right time and the right place.

His work was done here. After a quick cleanup—which is where his janitorial skills came in handy—the newest package would be ready for its special delivery.

Rodney hummed to the music. He enjoyed his job, not the one at the university, but this one here in his workroom. Sometimes it was backbreaking, standing over the bodies all day, but in the end, it was worth all the effort.

Chapter One

Traci Farris had been running for what seemed like miles. Running away from Jack Armstrong's apartment. Running away from what easily would have been an ugly confrontation with Jack's fiancée, Philippa Tannenbaum. Running away because she'd rather die than face Flippy and relive that look of shock and betrayal on her best friend's face.

"Wait," a man's voice called out. Traci turned toward the sound in midstride and nearly collided with a concrete bus bench.

Gasping for breath, she stopped short and grabbed the bench post for support while her heart raced to play catch-up with her feet. She just wanted to disappear, to be swallowed up by the earth as twilight settled like a shroud over the ghostly quiet town of Graysville.

The man at the bus stop—he was more of a big hulk of a boy—flashed her a dazzling smile that transformed his flabby face and lit up the night. It was a friendly face, and right now Traci desperately needed a friend. She'd seen him around campus from time to time. Hard to miss. He was very slow, but sweet, helpless, and harmless. He'd waved to her a number of times on her way to and from classes, and she'd waved back. She recalled helping him count out change once at the University bookstore.

The boy fixed her with an endearing look.

"Don't you remember? I saw you in the show. You signed your picture for me."

Puzzled at first, Traci suddenly remembered where she'd last seen the boy-man. He'd approached her after last year's homecoming pageant with his program in hand, asking for her autograph, just another star-struck fan, a backstage hanger-on. He'd been shy and appreciative when she signed his program. She'd been flattered. The boy had been lost in the crowd of people that night, agitated and confused when the cameras started flashing and the well-wishers surrounded her, almost crushing the two of them.

"I'm waiting for my brother to pick me up," the boy announced in a monotone. "He's late."

"I'm sorry," Traci managed, leaning against the post of the bus bench, still winded. "I really have to be going, but if you need to call your brother I have my cell phone right—" She realized then that she'd run out of Jack's apartment without her purse or her cell phone. She wasn't going back there anytime soon. "Well, I'm sure he'll be along soon," Traci said, happy to focus on someone else's problems for a moment. "But I've got to be going."

"Where are you going?"

Traci couldn't answer because she didn't know.

"I'm going to the end of the world," the boy announced, smiling.

Perhaps she hadn't heard him correctly. "The end of the world?"

"That's where I live," said the boy. "Here." He placed his right hand over his heart and then pointed a fat forefinger to a yellowing piece of paper pinned to his pitifully outdated flowered shirt. Didn't the boy own a coat? It was freezing outside. At least she'd had the presence of mind to grab hers before leaving the "scene of the crime." A Miami girl, born and bred in the sun, she hated the cold with a passion.

Traci followed the boy's black button eyes as they moved down insistently to the note. Did he want her to read it?

"My name is Donny Willis," she obliged. "I live at 5555 Skyline Road. Please take me home."

"You're real pretty," said Donny. "Just like my mama. My mama was real pretty, too."

"Thank you," Traci said, her heart beating back to a near-normal pace. "But I really need to go now."

"If my brother doesn't come, I'm supposed to take the bus."

Looking around, Traci suddenly felt exposed standing at the isolated bus stop as darkness got a chokehold on the sky. She'd passed a few stragglers, girls walking in pairs, scurrying home before curfew, probably packing heat. Normally the campus would have been alive with people. But nothing was normal anymore in Graysville. Every girl on campus was scared and wondering who the killer would grab next.

If she had her cell phone she could call one of her sorority sisters for a ride home. Or one of those walking or driving student-safe-escort services. Or 9-1-1. She looked around. There wasn't a pay phone or a policeman in sight. Where were the cops when you needed them?

But if she went back to the sorority house, Flippy would find her and demand an explanation. Her friend, her *former* friend, deserved an explanation. But Traci had no excuse for her actions.

A fresh set of hot tears streamed from Traci's eyes. Flippy had every right to hate her. Traci knew from the beginning she'd been wrong to poach what belonged to someone else. But she'd done it anyway.

Jack had been depressed about his football injury. He'd needed sympathy and a shoulder to cry on, and Traci had been more than available.

Tired of Jack's self-pity routine, Flippy was too busy now with her own life to babysit him. Once, she'd even let it slip to Traci that she wasn't sure she was doing the right thing by marrying Jack. That she'd waited so long for love to come along and it never had. That her mother had been thrilled when Jack finally proposed. Barbara Tannenbaum was a force of nature. Flippy had spent her entire life trying to please her mother, so she and Jack had set a date. But that could have been just girl talk, pre-wedding jitters. Jitters or not, Flippy's uncertainty didn't give Traci a license to steal. Or stab her best friend in the back.

It didn't matter that Traci had secretly nursed a crush on Jack from the moment Flippy had introduced them and that Jack had fanned the flames by flirting with her every chance he got, especially when Flippy's back was turned. One thing had led to another, and they'd become involved on the sly. And then Traci was in too deep, up to her neck in love with him. And now she'd lost them both.

Earlier that evening, Flippy had walked in on them in bed, and the whole house of cards had come crashing down. The last words she heard were Jack's, feebly begging Flippy to come back to him. He hadn't even been concerned about Traci's fragile feelings.

"Are you taking the bus?" Donny interrupted her

thoughts.

"No," Traci said softly, her eyes looking away from Donny's beady ones, her mouth closed clam tight, her breath coming now in rapid, shallow bursts.

"Will you wait with me?"

Traci shrugged and began to shiver. Her body had started to shut down after the adrenalin rush. She needed time to think about what to do next. Maybe riding the bus to the end of the world wasn't such a bad idea. No, it was a really stupid idea.

She contemplated bolting from the bench when the blue city bus screeched to a stop in front of them and the driver cranked open the heavy steel doors.

"Donny? Your brother late again? Hop on. I'll take you on home."

"He says he lives at the end of the world," Traci told the bus driver. "But there's an address pinned to his shirt."

The bus driver chuckled. "He's been wearing that raggedy old note for years. It's a wonder anyone can still read it. Says his mother wrote it. He lives at the last stop, the end of the bus line. He calls it the end of the world. Probably never been anyplace else."

"I want to wait for my brother," Donny said. "She can wait with me." The boy turned to face Traci and nudged her, creeping uncomfortably closer into her personal space.

"I—uh, need to go," said Traci, noticing that the full moon was on the rise.

"She can wait with me," Donny repeated.

Then Donny started to rock. Back and forth. And rant. And refused to get on the bus.

"Wait with me," Donny wailed, touching his face

over and over as tears puddled on his puffy cheeks. His nostrils flared and dripped and his pupils dilated. And he continued to rock, while remaining bolted to the ground.

"You a friend of Donny's or Rodney's?" asked the driver.

"I don't know any Rodney. He looked lost and I just wanted to help."

"Look, miss, sometimes he gets like this. And he won't stop. I hate to leave him here alone like this. No telling when that smart-ass brother of his will come back for him. But I have to keep to my schedule. Don't want to lose my job, do I? And you can't wait here. It's not safe for a pretty girl like you, what with everything that's going on around campus. You can ride along with us and I'll drop you where you need to go after I finish my route."

Traci shook her head hesitantly. Her every instinct told her it was definitely not a good idea.

"Please," Donny sniffled, sensing victory.

Mentally challenged or not, he was nothing but a big manipulative mama's boy, Traci realized as she started to ease away from the bus. But if Donny left, she'd be alone. That's what it came down to. She didn't want to get on the bus. Neither did she want to be alone.

"I might be able to stay for a few more minutes, just until his brother comes," Traci relented, although everything in her argued against it.

"Thanks, miss. Now be careful out here. Why don't you call the campus police to come pick you up, walk you home?"

Flippy worked for the campus police. Traci wouldn't be calling anybody in that place.

Donny wiped his eyes on his shirt sleeve and looked back at her with that hundred-watt smile, like everything was all right again in his world.

"You're pretty," Donny repeated. "Just like my mama."

The double doors closed with a loud whoosh, and the bus pulled away just as a green Thunderbird came roaring out of nowhere and pulled up in front of the bus stop.

"You're late," the boy accused, pointing his finger at the car, his fat face red and splotchy from crying.

"Sorry, bro. Hey, who's your pretty little girlfriend?"

Donny blushed and stammered. "Sh-she's not my girlfriend."

"Did the bus driver happen to get a look at your new girlfriend?" Donny's brother asked.

"I told you, she's not my girlfriend."

"Too bad."

Traci leaned into the car, trying to get a look at the man inside, but it was dark and the man turned his face away as he switched off his headlights. "I was afraid to leave your brother alone. He was really upset."

"She's beautiful *and* she's a Good Samaritan," said the driver. "We hit the jackpot this time, big bro. Get in the car, Donny. Say thank you to your pretty little girlfriend."

"She's not my girlfriend," Donny insisted as he opened the car door and lumbered into the front seat.

"Donny doesn't exactly have a way with words, does he?" mocked the faceless voice that floated from the car. "But I appreciate you waiting with my brother. I'd like to show my gratitude. Can I give you a lift anywhere?"

"N-no," Traci stammered. "Th-thank you. Goodbye, Donny." Traci edged away from the bus stop, gave a half-hearted wave, and started walking in the opposite direction of the car. The Thunderbird swerved, spun around in a cloud of dust and pulled up alongside her. A frisson of fear climbed up her spine and lodged in her brain. The car windows opened and the vehicle tracked Traci as she began to run.

The car kept rolling. Traci kept running. But she could still hear the man's voice.

"I offered you a ride home. Are you always this rude? Don't you know it's not safe to be out alone at night?"

Traci kept up her pace.

"Grab her, Donny. Your girlfriend needs a lesson in manners."

"But why?" the boy asked.

"Don't ask questions. Don't I always know what's best for you? We're just taking her home for a short visit. Wouldn't you like a little company? It gets pretty lonely with just us guys around the house way out at the end of the world."

"Don't hurt her."

"Now where would you get an idea like that? You watch too many movies, bro. Go ahead and get her, and be quick about it before someone else sees you."

Traci risked a peek back as Donny stepped out of the car. He was as big as a giant, but he moved quickly and he was gaining on her.

"No, please." Traci tried to shout, but the words came out as a strangled whisper. A sick knot of fear twisted in her throat, festered in the pit of her stomach, choking her as it rose into her mouth. A slick band of sweat glistened on her chest, pooled under her arms and froze there. Her knees buckled. Each breath tore out of her with the force of a jagged knife. But still she ran. She ran like her life depended on it.

Chapter Two

"Flippy, I mean Philippa, uh, Miss Tannenbaum, there's an Officer Luke Slaughter from the Graysville Police Department here to see you."

Despite her practiced calm, carefully cultivated from her beauty queen days, Flippy's stomach shuddered as a tremor rumbled through her body. The seismic shift seized her fragile heart. She had never expected to see Luke Slaughter again, much less this soon, fully clothed, and certainly not under these circumstances.

"Send him in, Misty."

Had she managed to keep the vibrating waves of tension from her voice? Just barely. She squeezed her eyes shut, remembering the last time she'd seen Luke Slaughter, bare and naked, sleeping beside her in her dump of an apartment. Actually, he'd had her in an unconscious octopus hold, hands everywhere, possessively clutching her body like so many tentacles, cutting off her circulation so she could barely breathe. At least it felt like she was suffocating. Had it only been a week ago? Could she face him here after what they'd done (what hadn't they done?), and after how shabbily she'd treated him when the night was over? Despite the nauseated feeling in her stomach, the answer was "yes," but it wouldn't be fun.

It was only her first day on the job as part of the

newly-created Campus-City Homecoming Homicides Task Force, and she wanted to make a good impression. So she couldn't hide under her desk, although that was her first inclination when she heard Misty announce Luke's arrival. But there was too much at stake for personal feelings to get in the way. They'd even called in Crystal & Hale, that new husband and wife team from the psychic detective agency in Atlanta. He was a former cop who had the misfortune of being named Jack, and she was that famous psychic, Crystal Ball Kate, who had accurately predicted the crash of Vince Rivers' private jet and helped solve the Midtown Atlanta and Sydney Strangler cases.

Her big opportunity was about to walk through the door, and she didn't intend to blow it. No matter how much it cost her personally. She'd just have to suck it up and remember who she was now—a professional, with her own office and her own receptionist.

She'd hired Misty Waters away from DaVinci's, the local pizza hangout next door to the nondescript, but affordable, campus police department annex. Hired her for her personality and her multitasking ability. She'd seen the girl juggle six tables of rowdy college kids without breaking a sweat or dropping a plate. She certainly hadn't hired her for her fashion sense, which seemed to be based on the concept that "less is more." Flippy's next order of business would be to persuade the ex-pizza tosser to upgrade her wardrobe and perhaps put on something more respectable and less *receptive*.

True, Misty might be a little rough around the edges, but Flippy could spot potential, and the girl had it with a capital "P." Misty would be okay as long as she focused on answering the phone and not giving visitors "The Works"—a bird's-eye view of her considerable toppings. Either way, she sincerely hoped hiring Misty Waters turned out to be a smart decision, because this case of murder and mayhem seemed to be spiraling out of control, and Flippy's phone wouldn't stop ringing.

As she looked up, Luke Slaughter backed into her office, magnificent butt first—his muscles straining under the weight of a large cardboard box. He turned to face her, while craning his neck back shamelessly in Misty's direction. There was something vaguely familiar about the shape of the man's butt. Or maybe it was that Dirty Harry-sized piece bulging out of his hip holster. Flippy tried to block out all thoughts about the night she'd just spent with Luke Slaughter. It wasn't difficult to do, since she had been so hammered and intent on revenge against her serial cheating ex-fiancé, Jack Armstrong.

No doubt about it, the man looked good in a uniform. And out of it. And he was a warm body. Sufficient qualifications at the time for a revenge fuck. Flippy suppressed rogue thoughts of that night. A night that refused to stop flashing before her eyes. The only thing clear about that night was that it had been a big mistake. A mistake she'd never make again.

"Damn, Flippy, I like the way you've decorated the place." Luke dropped the box on the floor, where it landed with an ungainly thud.

He wasn't even pretending to look at her office furniture, a ragtag cast of characters that shouted yard sale.

"If you're referring to Misty Waters, my

receptionist, you can just stop drooling."

"Misty Waters? You're kidding, right?"

"No, I'm not. She's intelligent and she works for *me*. Keep that in mind and stop entertaining your pathetic fantasies."

"Whoa, how about stowing the attitude, sweetheart." Luke's smile had vanished. "I didn't ask to work this case with you, but I'm ready to play nice."

"I *know* you didn't ask for this."

Flippy rose to her feet. "In fact, I *know* you bad-mouthed me to Chief Bradley, doing everything you could to keep me *off* the task force. I believe your exact words were, 'Chief, she may be easy on the eyes, but she's a bubble-headed beauty queen you can't count on in a crunch. She's not a particular fan of handguns. I wouldn't want to stake my life on her. She couldn't even last six days in law school.' Am I getting warm?"

Luke's cheeks paled, taking on the color of the New Dawn roses that wound around the trellis outside her office window. At least he had the decency to look embarrassed before he let loose with that lethal baby-face smile of his, which had a habit of appearing at the most inappropriate times. She still had dreams about those dangerous dimples.

"Don't even bother to deny it, you slimy little serpent," Flippy hissed. "When one of my friends filled in for your chief's secretary, she listened on the other side of the door when you tried to torpedo me."

"I was just blowing off steam."

"What you almost blew was my chance to do something meaningful with my life. To prove myself to my new director."

Luke's lips curled. "Old Iron Balls?"

"You think undermining me for what could possibly be the biggest assignment of my career is funny? And is it really necessary to insult my director? Elizabeth Beckham is a law enforcement legend."

"She's also a royal pain in the ass. Maybe I should call her *Queen* Elizabeth. No, I don't think it's funny, and yes, I think it's necessary to insult your director, because she's the scary bitch who fired me from the campus police department. But do you really think you're cut out for this kind of work?"

"I need this job and I can do this job, if you would just step out of my way."

"What's the worst crime you've ever dealt with?" Luke challenged. "Bicycle and backpack theft? That's a long way from serial killers."

"Try date rape and sexual assault," Flippy countered. "I'm the Department's Victim Services Advocate. It's my job to ensure that all victims of crime on campus receive fair treatment in accordance with the provisions of Florida State Statute 960."

"I know the statute, sweetheart, but you don't know Jack-shit about dealing with a serial killer."

Flippy fumed at what she knew was the intentional mention of her ex-fiancé's name.

"Why don't we leave Jack out of this?" She shot Luke a hostile glare.

"Gladly. But bottom line, you don't belong on this task force. This isn't some stupid beauty contest. You are not qualified to serve."

"I'm the new crisis manager on the task force," Flippy informed Luke. "You people have a major crisis on your hands. I'm *definitely* cut out for this kind of work, and I *do* belong here because my director wants me on the team. And what's so great about you, anyway? You're a part-time cop at a two-bit metro police department in a one-horse town. Don't you have any loftier aspirations?"

"I'm going to law school at night," Luke said, raising his chin defensively.

"Been there. Done that."

"That's right. Chief Bradley figured that since you and I went to law school together, *before* you flunked out after a whopping *six days*, we could team up on this case."

"Dropped out," she corrected. "Because we're such good buds, is that what you told him?"

"Look, Flippy..."

"And don't call me Flippy. My professional name is Philippa."

"What kind of name is Flippy anyway?" Luke challenged, plopping his lanky frame down on her only guest chair, which made annoying creaking noises every time he moved. "Wasn't that the name of a dolphin or something?"

"That was Flipper, and what business could that possibly be of yours?"

"Whoa, don't flip out on me," Luke protested, his eyes sparkling as he signaled time-out with his hands. "I'm just curious."

Trying to exercise a modicum of restraint in the spirit of cooperation, Flippy graciously answered, "It's a nickname. My baby sister couldn't pronounce Philippa."

Flippy. How many times had she been teased about her nickname? A name that had stuck throughout high school and college. *Flippy Longstocking. My Friend*

Flippy. Dippy Flippy. She didn't know any other Philippas, but how could her mother ever have thought that name was distinctive?

And how many times had Jack abused her name? His standard Valentine's Day card read, "I've flipped over you." And how could she ever forget his all-time favorite—"I'm hungry. Why don't you flip me some pancakes?" When he knew perfectly well that she couldn't even cook.

She had let Jack call her Flippy, but Jack was out of her life now, and no one was ever going to call her Flippy again.

"Bastard," she mumbled under her breath.

"Jesus, Flippy."

"Luke, you obviously can't follow instructions, so get your tight ass out of my chair."

Luke's eyebrows rose in amusement, but he didn't budge.

"I could return the compliment, but I'm a gentleman, so I won't. Luke eased the chair back on two legs and folded his hands in a leisurely manner behind his head.

Flippy wanted to grind his balls, one at a time, under the heel of her shoe until she forced that smug look off his face. But he was just winding up.

"How do you rate an office anyway?" said Luke, who'd already moved on to the next insult. "You just got this job."

"In the type of work I do, I need a separate space from the rest of the department. When I counsel victims, we sometimes discuss sensitive matters. They're traumatized enough without having the whole department listening in on our private conversations."

"And the way I see it, *you* need *me*. The city has jurisdiction in this case, and my chief backs me up on that."

"Well, according to my director, we have jurisdiction here. The bodies of the five victims were found on landmark sites around the campus, so you're on *our* turf. We were responsible for forensic examination of the crime scenes before the city started sticking its nose into our business. You're overstepping, Slaughter."

"*You're* the one who's overstepping," Luke argued. "The girls weren't necessarily murdered on campus, so it looks like jurisdiction is a muddy issue. Why don't you stop acting like a girl and stop trying to turn this into a tug-of-war over jurisdiction. We're supposed to be working together. That's why it's called a *joint* task force."

"You people couldn't solve a crime if the killer walked through this door and turned himself in."

"You act like it's your job to *solve* the crime. The way I understand it, your role is to manage the media and handle the families, help calm fears. Leave the investigation to the professionals."

"And you consider yourself one of the professionals?"

"I'm a police officer. Which is a damn sight better than calling in some psychics from Atlanta. Why the hell they did that, I'll never know. And isn't that former Atlanta cop named Jack something or other? What is it about you and guys named Jack? You seem to attract them like flies."

Flippy went after Luke with both barrels blazing. "Jack *Hale* and his *psychic* wife just solved the Sydney

Strangler case. What case have you solved lately? In fact, where were you last year when the homecoming queen you were *supposed* to be protecting was found stabbed to death in her dressing room at the stadium?"

Luke blanched, then bounced back with his best defensive move.

"You mean when I found *you, the first runner-up*, standing over her body? Way to kill the competition, Flip."

Flippy gnawed on her bottom lip. That was a scene she'd spent the last year and a half trying to forget. A scene that replayed over and over on a continuous feed in her head. A scene that apparently no one in this city would ever let her forget.

"They were calling for us to get in the car to circle the field," Flippy explained. "Everyone was there but Melinda. I was the one who went back to get her when you pulled your disappearing act. And sh-she was just lying there, curled up in a ball, in a pool of blood. And she wasn't moving. Sh-she was—"

"Is 'dead' the word you're looking for?"

"Yes. You were there. And history seems to be repeating itself."

"Maybe I ought to be asking *you* where *you* were the night Traci Farris went missing?" Luke said.

Flippy slumped against her seat, sucked in short breaths, and went silent. If anyone even suspected that she had been the last person to see Traci Farris before she disappeared, she would be pulled off the task force, maybe even arrested.

She had the unfortunate knack of always managing to be in the wrong place at the wrong time. Timing never was one of her strong suits. *She* knew she was innocent, but it wouldn't look that way to the FBI, who'd just been called in on the Homecoming Homicides case. She'd be the first person they would suspect. Again, she had motive. She'd walked in on Traci and her fiancé *in flagrante delicto*. And she had opportunity. But short of scalding them to death with a steaming pot of hot chicken soup, they wouldn't find a murder weapon. Because there was none.

If the authorities knew what had happened, they might go after Jack. But even though Jack was a cheating bastard, he hadn't killed Traci. He could hardly get out of bed. Which was the crux of the problem in the first place. But it wouldn't look good for either of them. That was one little secret she intended to keep to herself.

"Are you accusing me of something?" she managed.

Luke gave her a satisfied look.

"Should I be?"

"What you *should* be doing is trying not to veer off topic. We've got a crisis on our hands."

"I'll agree that this sadistic son-of-a-bitch has Graysville by the balls."

"Do you think the same guy who killed Melinda is killing the new crop of homecoming contestants?" That's something Flippy had long suspected. The Melinda Crawford murder was now a cold case. A serious blight on the record of the University police force. And a serious blight on her own reputation and Luke's.

"The FBI says no. Our guy is a serial killer. He wouldn't have killed that one time and then waited another whole year to kill again."

"But maybe he was locked up in prison, or maybe he has been killing in another state. Maybe he's tied to other unrelated murders we're not even investigating."

"You think we haven't thought of that? The FBI is looking into all those possibilities. They've considered all the angles. They don't need any advice from a novice."

"You're nothing but a rookie city cop."

"If I solve this case, I could make detective."

"That's disgusting, Luke. Climbing over dead bodies to get to the top."

Luke blinked, flexed his fingers, and gave Flippy a menacing and meaningful look.

"That's not what I'm doing," he said. "And what about you? You're interested in solving this case to restore your damaged reputation."

Flippy wanted to slap him, partially because it was true.

"I am trying to take back control of this situation," Flippy said, emphasizing each word, "which is what I do best."

"Situation" was a misnomer. It had quickly mushroomed into a full-blown crisis.

"Maybe you're right," Luke admitted. "This case is spinning out of control. We can use all the help we can get, even from a psychic, although I don't know what she's going to do—hold a séance and connect with the spirits of the dead girls to find out who killed them?"

"That's not even funny. We'll find out soon, won't we? They're driving down this afternoon for the press conference. The city is crawling with media. I need to know everything you know now, so I can be prepared when the reporters start shooting questions at me.

Unfortunately, they'll want all the gory details. Director Beckham has been handling the press so far, but she wants me up to speed. So hit me with those files. I want to start with the crime scene photos, then the police reports and the ME reports and photos. I assume that's what you've got in that box."

"Didn't know you were into blood and guts. You want photos? Fine."

Luke bent over, lifted a stack of files from the box on the floor, and stood up, deliberately pounding the manila folders on her desk, removing some graphic shots and displaying the gruesome photos for maximum effect, practically rubbing Flippy's nose in them.

Flippy felt the remains of the greasy doughnut she had downed for breakfast churning in her stomach and threatening to rise to the surface. She closed her eyes and fought to retain what was left of her dignity and the doughnut.

Dammit, Luke was expecting a reaction. It was just what she *didn't* want to happen. She was *not* going to lose her cool, she promised herself, or her breakfast.

But the message never made it to her brain. Like it or not, the doughnut, and whatever else she had in her stomach, was coming up. Barely managing an "Excuse me," she made a beeline for the bathroom in the outer office.

After that embarrassing episode, Flippy rinsed out her mouth with water. Then she splashed more water on her face until the room stopped spinning and she could catch her breath. Just as she had regained her composure, Misty walked into the bathroom.

"Hey, Flippy, are you okay? You don't look so hot. Can I get you anything?"

"I'm fine, Misty. It must have been that greasy doughnut I ate this morning."

"And talk about looking hot, can I just say Officer Luke Slaughter is one great-looking guy?"

"No, you may not."

"And it's not just that he's packing heat," Misty added. "But he does have quite a package, if you know what I mean."

"For Pete's sake, this is a place of business. Could you please get that phone? I'll be fine."

Misty sashayed out of the bathroom.

When Flippy returned to her office, Luke had strategically spread out the rest of the photos in glorious, gory detail across her desk.

"Flip, you look a little peaked. Why don't you go and lie down on that bad excuse for a couch over there while I finish arranging these photos. I'm available if you need some company."

Flippy tried a breathing exercise to calm herself down, but it was too late for that.

"All right, you immature rat bastard, listen up. I am going to pick up the phone and have you reassigned. It's obvious we can't work together if you can't get over yourself. Okay, we had sex. Let's just get that out on the table."

"Great sex," Luke corrected, "on the table, under the table."

Okay, great sex, Flippy had to admit, hazy as that night had been, trying hard not to picture Luke's first-class ass naked on her kitchen table, her fingernails digging into his flesh. Had it only been one week ago that Luke had rocked her world? That much she did remember.

She also remembered the humiliation of the morning after. She'd been hurting, but all she'd accomplished was to end up looking like an easy lay and embarrassing herself with Luke. Luke was a great guy and a good friend, and she'd blown it by jumping in the sack with him when things had gone wrong with Jack. He had to think she was the lamest woman in the world. And he'd be right.

"I was mad at Jack and I got back at him. I was drunk."

"You were wasted and I was handy."

"I'm sorry, okay?"

"Yeah, I got the message loud and clear the next morning when you told me what we did was a big mistake and not to ever tell anyone it happened."

"Get it together and man up, Luke," said Flippy, trying to hide her discomfort behind a trail of laughter.

"You think what we did together was funny? That's not how I remember it. But hey, okay, if that's the way you want to play it. It was only a one-night bang."

Luke fixed Flippy like a laser with his dangerously frosty green eyes, while she blinked stupidly. He looked more like a fierce warrior. He could be gentle, she remembered, but there was no sign of *that* Luke here.

"As far as I'm concerned, it never happened," Luke added. "And, just so you know, I was lying to spare your feelings. That night was completely forgettable. You beauty queen types are highly overrated."

Flippy's shoulders slumped forward.

"It was a mistake for both of us, then," she mumbled.

"You made that pretty clear when you wouldn't

return my phone calls. How was I supposed to know you were still 'All Jacked Up.' "

"I'm over Jack," Flippy insisted, averting her glance, doing her best to avoid looking at Luke or the photos.

Okay, even if Luke was a weasel, Flippy was still ashamed of her behavior. Jack had been unfaithful and she had desperately wanted to prove she could play the same game. She'd picked Luke, played Luke, because he had been available and—Misty was right—he *was* hot. And she knew he wanted her. And had for a long time. He could try to play it cool, but he wasn't very good at hiding his feelings.

And it worked both ways. She'd actually daydreamed about Luke in criminology class as an undergraduate, and those six days in law school, anticipating what it might be like to be with him. She'd been stunned to the core that the reality was so much better than anything she'd ever imagined.

But even if she could forgive Luke for badmouthing her to his chief, *and* to her director, after their little interlude, it was never a good idea to mix business with pleasure. Even mind-blowing, earth-shattering pleasure. Apparently, he hadn't felt the same way.

Flippy raised her gaze to Luke's thunderous face.

"How many times do I have to apologize, Lucas? You have every right to be mad at me. But can you work with me or not? This isn't about us, okay? Those aren't just some anonymous faces in these pictures. I know—knew—these girls. They've been butchered by some madman who is still out there and who probably won't quit until all thirty girls who were in the pageant are dead. And nobody seems to have a clue as to who he is and how to stop him. I want this case solved as much as you do. Now *can* you work with me?"

Luke leveled his eyes at hers again, and what she saw there was undetectable. Nothing, zilch, nada. She didn't have the slightest idea in hell what the man was thinking. Did he want to skewer her or screw her? "Take your pick" was what she was reading. Maybe a little of both.

"Like I said, no big deal. It's already forgotten," Luke said coolly as he headed to his car to bring in another box of files. His voice was steady, but there was plenty of venom there. He was never going to get over what had happened between them. And she could understand just where he was coming from. Because the same thing had happened to her with Jack.

Jack Armstrong had always been the one with the life plan. He had his priorities straight. Star running back for the North Florida University football team, his strategy was to win the Heisman trophy, enter the NFL, make a boatload of bucks, and probably sleep with every cheerleader on both coasts and everywhere in between, if he could manage it. Some of those were actually worthy goals.

But when he'd torn his ACL at the homecoming game, that was the end of Jack's life plan, his confidence, *and* their relationship. Because two people who don't know where they're going aren't going to get very far.

Flippy was supposed to be the expert in crisis management. But right now, her entire life was one big crisis she could barely manage.

She'd run headlong into a brick wall last week

when Jack went into self-destruct mode, cheated on her, and ripped out her heart. She was still not over him. For four years she'd thought he was her future, but that promise was all shot to hell.

Luke had been right about one thing. She'd only lasted six days in law school, probably some kind of collegiate record. But that was par for the course for her. One thing she understood now was that she had never come first with Jack. And she never came first in anything.

So how did she manage to get involved with the biggest murder case in Graysville, Florida, certainly in the South, maybe even in the entire country? The case the tabloids were calling The Homecoming Homicides.

When Director Beckham mentioned to Chief Bradley that a girl on her staff had been first runner-up on last year's NFU homecoming court and was director of this year's homecoming pageant, where she'd worked with all the dead and missing girls, bingo— Flippy was recruited.

Why?

One, because Luke Slaughter thought he'd throw her a bone by offering to work with her, and probably hoped to jump her bones again, which was never going to happen. Two, because she was a former contestant herself, the chief and her director reasoned that she fit the profile of the victims. Apparently, it was important to profile the victims as well as the perp because knowing the victims might help the police determine who might have access to them. And three, they were obviously out of options if they were looking in her direction.

The thing was, the murder investigation had

stalled. The campus and city police forces had hit a roadblock in the Homecoming Homicides case after three months of fruitless and frustrating investigation, and the death toll of beauty pageant contestants continued to rise. The FBI had been salivating to gain access, and now that they were involved on the task force, the university and the city police departments were forced to beef up their efforts or lose total control of their case.

They needed a spokesperson to bring down the curtain on the media circus—a sexy body to put a pretty face on a terrible tragedy, someone to take attention off the half-assed job they were doing and make them look good, since they seemed incapable of actually catching the bad guy. If they chose to put their faith in an ex-homecoming queen runner-up with questionable crime-solving credentials, who was she to argue?

She may not be a winner, but she was going to make something of her runner-up life and succeed in solving this case because she had to. And not just because time was running out but because she was the last person to see the missing girl, Traci Farris, alive. And because, more than anything, she'd wanted her dead.

Chapter Three

Luke had worked up a full head of steam by the time he'd hoisted the second box of files out of the trunk of his car. Who did that bubble-headed blonde think she was? And what was she thinking? Rubbing his nose in the fact that she'd only slept with him to get back at that frat-boy all-star jack-off boyfriend of hers. Drowning her sorrows by crawling into bed with the first guy who came along, *now,* in Graysville, when the killer could have been watching her, hunting her? Waiting for his next opportunity? Was she even thinking at all? Obviously not. Did she even have a brain in that ditzy little head of hers?

What if he hadn't been there? What if it had been someone else she'd taken home with her? He'd had a thing for her forever. She didn't have a clue. He'd known from the first time he set eyes on her that they could be good together. But with Jack in the picture, he didn't stand a chance. He watched out for her that night in the bar. He kept her from leaving with another guy. He thought it could be the start of something new, something great. He'd been waiting for his opportunity forever. He knew she wasn't the kind of girl who slept around, but she was acting crazy that night. She was buzzed, that's for sure. High on hatred for Jack, maybe. But she wasn't herself. And, of course, he took advantage. But he did it for her own good. Better him than someone else. At least that's how he rationalized his behavior.

He felt guilty about taking her back to her apartment, but hey, she was on the hunt that night, he reminded himself. Luke simply decided to make sure he was the one she snagged.

He told her the night had been forgettable, but for him it was anything but. He'd played that night over and over in his mind this past week. Would he have done anything different? He tried to satisfy her, thought he had. But it was doubtful she even remembered what happened.

It was hardly a magical night for her. How could it be, when she was so drunk he had to carry her out to the car over his shoulder, in a fireman's hold, like a sack of potatoes. And he wanted her so much they didn't even get as far as the bedroom. They stripped each other naked and had at it on top of her kitchen table. Hardly memorable.

He wanted a do-over, a chance to rock the room. And he'd been patient, considerate. He let her sleep it off. Stayed up all night watching her sleep, hardly believing his luck, hardly believing she had actually let him take her home. She was as fragile as glass. He touched her hair and her beautiful face while she slept, softly brushing his lips against hers, wanting her to feel him even though she was practically comatose.

He knew he wasn't even in her league. All those times in criminology class, he couldn't stop looking at her. But she couldn't see him. She was too in love with the big football hero. Jack Armstrong—Jack of all trades, master of everything.

And then when Luke ended up on protective duty

for the homecoming court at the big game, he couldn't keep his mind off her, which inflamed another part of his body, which is why he'd had to take that quick bathroom break to relieve himself before escorting the homecoming court's vehicle around the field at halftime.

He'd been gone no more than ten minutes, and by the time he came back all hell had broken loose. The homecoming queen had gone missing, and Flippy, the first runner-up, was nowhere to be found. Until he hunted her down and found her standing over Melinda Crawford's dead body. Which is when his police training kicked in, his feelings flew out the window, and he started questioning her—accusing her, really.

And since no one else in the stadium knew what was going on, the game started back up and Jack Armstrong got injured. Flippy heard the play-by-play and sailed past Luke to run out onto the field to be with Jack, which made her look guilty as hell for leaving the scene of the crime before the police had a chance to question her. And things had gone downhill from there. She was cleared, but the papers had done a nice smear job on her and, just like that, she was out of his life forever. Until he'd spent six days sitting next to her in law school. And spent their first time in bed together last week.

She had definitely lost her way. He'd kept track of her. She'd tried everything, but nothing stuck. She only lasted six days in law school and no sooner had they reconnected than he lost her all over again. Not that he ever had her in the first place.

When she came up to him at the bar last week, he couldn't believe she had even noticed him, not in that way. And when she came on to him—

Luke's face colored just thinking about it. He hadn't been imagining it. Flippy had blatantly offered her body to him. She didn't have to try very hard, either. He was so hungry for her he could hardly help himself.

He should have known something was not right when she said she just wanted to have some fun and started to prance around her apartment performing a strip tease to an imaginary beat.

Then the next morning she mumbled something about how she'd appreciate it if he didn't tell anyone about any of this, forget it had even happened. A mistake, is what she had called it. She'd only acted that way (like a little slut), because she was getting back at her cheating boyfriend and she was drunk.

Even then, he'd wanted to do it with her again, in the worst way, but hey, he had his pride. She was just filling in the blanks for a missing boyfriend. And he was nobody's back-up plan.

He had a job to do. He was assigned to pick her brain, find out if she knew anything important about the night of the homecoming pageant, anything that could help the task force break the case. And his chief had charged him with wrestling the case away from the rookie campus police—the "coed cops" the guys at the station called them—and back into the hands of the city where it belonged. The FBI had already been called in, but he figured they had about one more week before the Feebs totally took over. And then he'd be shut out and lose his chance to make things right.

If he had been on the job, been where he was supposed to have been, he would have caught the killer

35

before he killed Melinda Crawford. He'd been reduced to handing out parking tickets to students who were illegally parked on campus. His career was in the toilet. But then Chief Bradley had relented, had taken a chance on him by hiring him on the city's police force, and agreed when he pleaded to be put on the Homecoming Homicides task force.

Right now the city and the campus cops both claimed a weak jurisdictional right to the case, but as the death toll climbed and the grief of the bereaved parents bled into every living room in the world, their jurisdictional argument wasn't going to stick—it was as transitory as ice cubes melting in a glass of warm beer on a sweltering summer day. And just as irrelevant, he knew.

But they weren't going to lose this case on his watch. Chief Bradley was counting on him, and he wasn't going to let down the chief or the City of Graysville—or himself, for that matter. The chief had shown a lot of confidence in him, putting him on the task force in the first place, and he had given his word.

One thing he was sure of. Flippy was hiding something. She could hardly look him in the eye. And he was damn sure going to dig until he discovered her secret, if he had to destroy her in the process.

Chapter Four

"Any news about Traci Farris?" Flippy asked nonchalantly as Luke sauntered back into her office, hefting a second cardboard box.

"No, except she's been missing for almost a week now."

Luke didn't have to spell out the significance of that statement. She'd wanted Traci out of her life and now poof, she'd disappeared and was gone, maybe forever. Blinking back tears, Flippy avoided looking at Luke so he wouldn't sense her discomfort. She knew she was partially responsible for Traci's predicament. If it hadn't been for her, Traci would never have run out of Jack's apartment and straight into the arms of a serial killer. Flippy had gone over and over it in her mind. And every way she sliced it, she was the guilty party.

Traci had been her shadow. Flippy had taken her former sorority sister under her wing, introduced her around to everyone. They had shared everything—even, it turned out, Flippy's fiancé.

Last week, when Flippy showed up unexpectedly at Jack's apartment to bring him a pot of chicken soup and boost his sagging spirits, she'd caught the two of them in bed. Nothing that night about Jack's spirit or his super-sized body part was even remotely sagging.

She remembered standing there like an idiot because she couldn't process the picture right there in front of her. Jack lying naked except for his lightweight knee brace, which ran from mid-thigh to mid-calf, and Traci only scantily clad in a Victoria's Secret Plunge Multi-Way Bra and V-string concoction, doing multiple things to Jack that Flippy had never even done.

"Jack?" She remembered calling his name, from what sounded to her like the bottom of an echo chamber, as she tried to work out an explanation in her head for what she was seeing. But the situation was exactly as it seemed. Shocked, Traci had shot out of bed, grabbed her clothes, and rushed past her into the bathroom without saying a word.

Jack had just looked at Flippy, looked right through her, really. No explanation. No apology. His eyes were glazed over. Later on, in one of the gazillion rambling phone messages he'd left her, he maintained he was knocked out on pain medication and under the influence. But drunk, drugged out, or not, there was no acceptable explanation for what he and Traci had been doing to each other, or had done to her.

Then she'd dropped it. Literally. Dropped the steaming pot of chicken soup she'd spent the whole day making, staining the creamy white carpet like a stream of urine. She had been so proud of herself. She'd found the recipe on the Internet and had gone to the grocery store to shop for fresh ingredients to make the broth from scratch. She'd lovingly cut up the carrots, onions, celery, and a parsnip, and even added a real roasting chicken, imagining how she would cook for Jack when they were married.

In return, she'd been rewarded with a rude slap in the face. A wake-up call. Later, when she rehashed that scene in her mind, she was sorry she hadn't poured the scalding soup all over the bastard's head.

Faced with the betrayal of her two best friends, Flippy was numb, heartsick, then flat out furious as the last few months of their relationship flashed through her brain like a B-movie. The agony she'd felt when she heard the announcer call the play-by-play when that defensive player came in low and took Jack out just as he was cutting back. The months of slavish devotion she'd lavished on Jack after his sports injury, during every stage of his long, hard road to recovery—the swelling, the surgery, the crutches, the physical therapy, the endless complaints that his career, and therefore his life, was over.

Hearing, and ignoring, or discounting, the countless times Jack had told her how *hot* he thought Little Sister Traci was. Apparently her own sympathy wasn't a big enough turn-on for him. He needed more adoration to pump up his sagging ego. Jack knew Flippy's history with her father. He knew that cheating was the one thing Flippy would not tolerate. She could understand head-butting and jump-up body bumping during a football game, but she refused to put up with any ass-grabbing off the field. She was too smart to subscribe to the tired explanation that "boys will be boys." How long had the betrayal been going on? What a laugh Traci and Jack must have had at her expense.

If she'd stayed in Jack's bedroom a moment longer she would have lost control. So, after she'd dropped the pot of soup, she turned around and walked out Jack's door and dropped out of his life forever. That was the last time she had seen Traci. Traci must have been taken that night, probably in the process of either coming after her to try to explain or trying to put as much distance between them as she could.

Traci would have left Jack's apartment alone. Jack couldn't have been much help in his condition. It was as if Traci had disappeared into thin air. No one had heard from her since that night.

Jack wasn't being accused of anything. The police had no reason to make a connection between Jack and Traci's disappearance. No one even knew that Traci had been in his apartment. No one but Flippy. And she was still too traumatized, and too embarrassed, to talk about the incident. To anyone. Especially not to Luke.

"Is there anything you can remember?" Luke's voice invaded her thoughts.

"Remember?" she asked blankly. That scene wasn't likely one she'd ever forget.

"About the pageant?" Luke prompted.

What did she remember about the night of the pageant? Following the intermission, they had presented the Miss Congeniality award and announced the six finalists. After the judges posed additional questions to the finalists, they'd narrowed down the field to the top three contestants who would comprise the homecoming court. The three candidates would ride in the homecoming parade and round the field in a sports car at halftime on game day when they would crown the queen. That was to be the last ride the homecoming queen would ever take, except in a hearse to the cemetery. Next to die was the first runner-up, followed by the second runner-up. It wasn't long after that the other pageant finalists started ending up dead too, one after the other.

Flippy paused, trying to refocus her mind on the night of the pageant. As pageant director, she'd spent the final moments before the curtains went up backstage with the contestants, and she could still recall their voices.

"Zip me up, Flippy."

"Help me with my pearls."

"Did I go overboard on the makeup?"

"Do these earrings go with my gown?"

"Flip, do these shoes make me look too tall?"

She had been in their shoes. Now, calming fluttering nerves and backstage jitters was her specialty. Nothing out of the ordinary stood out in her mind, *except the girls*. They were all extraordinary.

Suddenly another memory surfaced.

"There were cameras, Luke. Someone was shooting a DVD of the show the entire time the girls were on stage. I've got a copy right here in my office, if you want to take a look."

Flippy could see by the way Luke's face shifted he hadn't known about the video.

"Hell, yes, I want to see it. From now on, we share everything, got it? No secrets."

"Honesty works both ways, you know."

Flippy lowered her eyelids and bit her lower lip as she queued up the DVD. The memories broke like an avalanche in her mind. She thought about how agonizing it would be for the parents of the dead and missing girls to watch their beautiful daughters on screen, watch faces they would no longer see except in their memories—freeze-framed forever. Why did it always seem more tragic when the victims were beautiful?

"Who produced this video?" Luke demanded. "I want to see the raw footage, the parts that were scrapped. Everything that was shot."

"The pageant office probably hired a firm or a freelancer to shoot the event. Let me call my contact there, and then you can run a search on the company and the person who shot the video."

Unbelievable. How could the Graysville city police, who had tried to wrestle the investigation right out from under their campus counterparts, have overlooked such critical evidence? What else hadn't they thought of that was material to the case?

"The video would have panned the audience," Flippy said. "Someone in that audience is the killer or knows the killer."

"Fresh eyes," Luke said. "I was right about you bringing a fresh set of eyes to the investigation."

"You had something nice to say about me to your chief?" Flippy said, her suspicions still lingering.

"I'm not the bad guy here, Flip, and I think you know that."

Why was Luke being so cooperative all of a sudden? Was he planning to play nice and catch her off guard before he pounced? Luke made her nervous. He was always demanding something, something she couldn't give, wasn't ready to give. He hadn't been so nice when he'd marched her down to police headquarters, hands jerked roughly behind her back, to be questioned like a criminal after Melinda Crawford's murder.

Even though Luke had screwed her in more ways than one, this case could make her career. And to do that she needed to cooperate, no matter how uncomfortable he made her feel.

"Did you get a list of people who bought tickets to

the pageant, so you can trace them back through their credit cards or checks?" Flippy asked.

Most of the people in the audience had been VIPs or parents or friends of the contestants. Many had been from sororities or fraternities who sponsored the girls in the pageant. But one of those guests was a serial killer in sheep's clothing who had joined an unsuspecting audience in the auditorium with the vilest intentions.

"We're on that," Luke reported, "but what if the killer snuck in?"

"No chance. That place was locked down tight. Security wasn't letting anyone in without a ticket, even family members. I'm sure the video will give us some clues to help us solve the case."

"You're probably right," Luke agreed. "But like I said, it's not *your* job to solve the case."

"If I'm going to be effective, I've got to live and breathe this case."

"Okay," Luke relented, but Flippy could tell he was just placating her.

"Luke, the guy knew a video was being made, probably ordered one, and got turned on watching the girls over and over, the girls he killed or is planning to kill. I'll also get you the list of the people who ordered the video."

"That would be great."

Flippy turned out the lights, loaded the VCR, and she and Luke took their seats and started watching the video.

As the lights on the screen went down, a ghostly hush fell over the auditorium as the music rose and the girls took the stage for their opening number. It was "Razzle Dazzle" from *Chicago*. They had rehearsed for two months straight. Flippy had taken a disparate group of sorority girls who each marched to the beat of her own drummer and drilled them into a top-rate dance troupe that would be at home on any Broadway stage. The girls, lock-stepping in their sleeveless, knee-length black crepe dresses and matching high-heeled shoes, twirled rhythmically around the stage in tandem, wowing the crowd.

Any one of them could have made the cut to the final three and ascended to homecoming court. Of course, Flippy had her favorites. She knew what the judges were looking for, and though all the contestants had something, five or six of them had that special "It" quality, that grace, and enough style to take them into the winner's circle. She knew it the moment they walked into the spotlight. Hard to believe that almost every one of her original top picks was already dead.

And one, her own sorority sister and best friend, was missing and presumed dead. Even if Traci were still alive, the killer had her now and she was probably wishing she were dead. Any minute now someone would find her body. Flippy felt it in her bones. How had this happened? Why did it continue to happen? Since she was responsible for Traci's disappearance, she needed to help stop this killing spree, and make things right between them again, if it wasn't too late.

"Philippa?" Luke's serious voice cut into her thoughts and she felt his gentle tap on her shoulder. The video had stopped and she hadn't been concentrating. She'd have to watch it again, scan the audience for something she might have missed.

"Are you okay?"

Flippy wiped away the tears she hadn't realized she

was shedding, cleared her throat, and tried to focus on Luke's face. She didn't want his pity. She had something to prove to him and to Chief Bradley and Director Beckham, who had placed such trust in her. She desperately needed to demonstrate some semblance of professionalism. But professionalism had gone out the door the day she got assigned to this case. The situation had become extremely personal.

"Of course I'm not okay," Flippy said. "And I won't be okay until we find the man who did this. What motivates a person to do something like this?"

Luke shrugged his shoulders. "Serial killers commit murder for almost any reason. Maybe our guy was rejected by a beautiful girl one too many times in his life. When it comes to human behavior, almost anything is possible. Maybe he wants to make a name for himself. He did leave a signature."

"A signature?" Flippy asked. "Is that like an MO?"

"Signature is the thing the killer is trying to accomplish," Luke explained. "MO is the method of accomplishing it. The MOs in this case differ as they often do in serial killings. He kills each girl in a different manner. But the signature is always the same. In this case the dump site. He always dumps the bodies in well-known locations on campus.

"And in every case the left side of the victim's face is burned, pre-mortem. Our killer may have been obsessed, but he didn't take anything of real value from the victim. Not their money or their good jewelry. Maybe some trinket or keepsake we don't know about. Just part of her face, her identity. In essence, he robbed her of her beauty. None of this gets out to the media, understood? We're telling the public only what they need to know right now. We have to hold back certain facts that only the killer would know. That's standard procedure."

"I know how the game is played. But it's always best to be honest with the press. Once you realize there's a risk, you should go ahead and put it out there. Otherwise both of our departments could get sued and we'd be putting more girls at risk."

"But first we have to figure out what is driving the killer," Luke explained. "We have to determine if he knew his victims or if they were strangers. Even if they were strangers, there is probably a personal connection. Maybe the girls reminded him of someone he knew, or their behavior reminded him of someone or something he hates. You knew all the girls. What's your take?"

"It sounds like he hates beauty queens," Flippy reasoned.

"It seems that way," Luke said. "But why? If we can figure that out, it could lead us to the killer. Let's review what we do know." Luke began ticking off the facts.

One year later, another homecoming queen had been found dead in the stadium right before she was due to be crowned at the homecoming football game, and one girl from the homecoming court almost every week since had gone missing and then been found dead days later. It had stopped when the girls headed for home over winter break.

"The killer could be a student," Flippy said.

"We thought of that."

Apparently the Graysville police force wasn't too swift in the brains department. It had taken some time before the police even started putting the pieces together that all the girls were homecoming contestants. They had labeled the first death a random crime and the second a horrible murder. They were on their way to explaining away the third as another unfortunate tragedy when Flippy finally connected the dots and realized the murders weren't coincidental or unrelated.

"The newspaper says the Graysville police have strong leads and that you've conducted interviews with persons of interest. What can you tell me about that?"

Luke shifted in his seat, causing the chair to creak under his weight. "The truth?"

"No, I want you to lie to me. I can't help you if you're not honest with me. What do you have?"

Luke turned serious. "Honestly, we're coming up empty. The only lead we had was a city bus driver who went missing last week, the same night as Traci Farris disappeared. It's probably totally unrelated to the case, but we found the burned out hulk of a city bus in a deserted field outside of town, but the bus driver was not on the bus. His wife reported him missing. He was just about to retire. His disappearance doesn't make any sense. But it's the only reported crime in the city other than the murders, so we're looking into it for crossover possibilities. The chief thinks that if we find him he may be the key to solving this thing.

"Otherwise, we've got nothing to go on. Nothing that connects the girls except the fact that they were all homecoming contestants and their bodies were all dumped on campus. It's not about one girl now, it's about all of them. We don't know if the first murder was premeditated or if the killer saw the girls in the pageant and snapped. We don't know anything about the killer or what motivated him.

"We do know something about the victims, though," Luke continued. "All extraordinarily beautiful. All relatively the same age, and most were blonde and tall."

At this point Luke looked over at Flippy and left what passed between them unspoken. She was blonde and tall.

There was no need to describe herself. She was a typical Tri Delt. To most of the world that meant: Blonde, Beautiful, Bimbo. Of course she was blonde, and she'd *almost* won enough beauty contests to give credence to the fact that she was considered beautiful, but she drew the line at being called a bimbo. That was just the undeserved reputation the Tri Delts had to live with. Because, all in all, they were a pretty bright bunch. And they'd gone far in the world.

"Whoever he is, he's obviously getting off on this. But we have no motive, nothing to go on except that he is a serial killer," Luke said.

"How do you know that?"

"The FBI defines a serial killer as someone who commits three or more murders with a cooling-off period in between. In this case, except for winter break, the cooling off period has been brief, just a week or so."

"What about sexual assault?" Flippy asked, not sure if she really wanted to hear the answer.

"No sign of that. He doesn't kill for sex. There were injuries to the face, but no semen or evidence of molestation. I don't think it's about lust. That isn't what he's after. More like bloodlust. He's angry at something, that's for sure, because the violence is escalating. We think maybe he's sexually impotent, or maybe he's afraid or intimidated by the beauty of his victims. But he is enjoying what he's doing, and he could feel sexual excitement on some perverted level. Probably an antisocial personality. Couldn't have much of a conscience."

"Does he even feel remorse?" Flippy wondered. "He definitely feels something, or why else would he have killed those innocent girls?"

"He may have felt guilt with his first victim. But once he killed the first girl, he passed a point of no return and may feel he has nothing to lose. What's one more body, or thirty, for that matter? Those are questions we've been asking ourselves."

"Did you interview all the parents, all the friends of the girls?" Flippy was stating the obvious, but the less than stellar record of the task force to date demanded she cover all the bases.

"Of course we did. We had to rule out known suspects first, and boyfriends, or past boyfriends. We wanted to know about family troubles, and did anyone have an interest in any of the girls, especially if she didn't return those feelings? So far, all we've run into are dead ends."

And dead girls, Flippy couldn't help but thinking.

She hadn't been interviewed. No one from the force had asked about her whereabouts or her ex-boyfriends. She hoped Luke hadn't made the connection between herself and Traci and Jack. That was the last thing she wanted to discuss with him or anyone else. She didn't want to impede the investigation, but she knew Jack had nothing to do with Traci's disappearance. She still wasn't ready to trust Luke with that information.

"Has it occurred to you that if you follow the girls

it will lead you to the killer?" she suggested.

"Look, Flip—, Philippa, we're doing all we can."

"Are you staking out the landmarks at the college? That's where he's dumping the bodies. It's a pattern. The killings may have taken place at another location, but this guy obviously knows the NFU campus—Alice Springs, Richert Hall, Centennial Tower. Which adds more fuel to my theory that he might be a student or a former student. At least it tells me he's local versus out-of-town. Sooner or later a body's going to show up at another high-profile location. Major Peyton Stadium would be an obvious choice."

The stadium was recently renamed after the university's star quarterback of the same name, who'd died tragically in a pileup on the interstate on his way home during Thanksgiving break. Major Peyton had been Jack's best friend, which probably had, as much as anything, contributed to Jack's downward spiral and the injury that now defined him. Even before the injury, Jack had been inconsolable because his friend had been killed during the height of the season. The two had been inseparable. Jack caught Major's passes and they backed each other up on and off the field. Major had been Jack's wingman, and when that shining star was extinguished, Jack disappeared down a black hole and couldn't or wouldn't climb back out.

"Maybe he spends time at the scene after he dumps the bodies, enjoying what he's done. Time that could be spent catching the son of a bitch," Flippy speculated.

Luke looked interested. The city police obviously hadn't even thought in that direction.

They were a bunch of bozos, Keystone Kops, Flippy thought. Whether or not they were willing to admit it, they *did* need her help.

Luke read her thoughts. "Look, it's not like we don't know what we're dealing with here, but there's so little evidence, we're running out of leads."

"Did you ever think that maybe this guy was turned down by the university? Every year we receive some 29,000 applications and only 2,000 students are admitted in the entering class. You need to run that."

"That's a great idea," Luke said. "I'll tell the chief."

"And take credit for my ideas?"

"What does it matter who gets the credit if we catch the killer?"

"There goes my Mr. Nice Guy theory."

"You were part of the pageant," Luke said, ignoring Flippy's sarcasm. "And you were on the homecoming court the year before. Have you ever thought that the killer might be targeting you?" Luke asked.

Flippy sighed. Of course that thought had crossed her mind and was seriously creeping her out. A clean sweep. Maybe she had inadvertently seen the killer before he'd murdered Melinda Crawford and he wanted to tie up loose ends? Maybe *she* was one of those loose ends?

"I can offer you protection," Luke stated.

"I don't need a bodyguard."

"Because you're such a crack shot? Do you even own a handgun?"

"Why would I want to own a handgun? And I don't need you in my business. Don't you have a partner? I thought you guys usually travel in pairs."

"I have a partner, and he spells me when I'm in

class. He's my backup. But the chief put me on babysitting duty until this case is solved."

"Babysitting duty? Is that what you consider this? Look, Luke, we're equal partners."

"Call it what you want. We're stuck together until this thing is over. So I *will* be protecting you. You don't go out on patrol with me unless I okay it. You don't get near anything dangerous. You stay in the background where you belong."

Flippy was tempted to say, "Nobody puts Flippy in the background." But she thought better of it.

Instead, she said, "That's outrageous."

"I'm just looking out for you."

"I don't *need* you looking out for me."

"Don't worry. It's nothing personal. I'm assigned to you. I'm just doing my job. And if you know what's good for you, you'll get the hell out of my way and let me do it."

Flippy was speechless. She'd rarely heard Luke swear.

"Sorry," Luke growled.

"You don't *look* sorry. And you don't *sound* sorry."

"I'm just on edge. Anyway, we're getting off track here. Did you notice anything that didn't smell right the night of the pageant? Do you recall seeing anyone strange hanging out before the pageant or after?"

"I don't recall anything unusual. At least nothing that would justify someone killing or trying to kill all the girls."

Flippy rubbed her head. All this concentrating had given her a whale of a headache.

"Wait a minute, Luke. I do remember something,"

Flippy said, popping the last two aspirin from the bottle in her desk drawer.

"You okay?" Luke look concerned.

"I'm fine, but I do remember that there was someone, a young man, more of a boy, really, but big, who approached me at the end of the program. He was slow, I think, a little off, something about him wasn't quite right. But he was perfectly harmless. He came up to ask for my autograph. He said he wanted to get all the girls' autographs for his program. I thought it was kind of sweet, you know. He was so thrilled to talk to us. He had a killer smile. Very disarming. Could that be important?"

"Do you remember what he looked like? Did you see many autographs on his program?"

"It was months ago."

"Come on, Philippa. This could be critical. It could be the break we need. You don't think he was a student?"

"He'd be a little old to be a student," Flippy answered, struggling to remember something about the man that might prove material to the case. "He looked to be in his late twenties. But after talking to him, I'd say no way was he student material. He had a professional-looking camera hung around his neck. He wore a flowery shirt and really high pants stretched across his stomach, like he was channeling Steve Irkle. But he wasn't an official member of the press. He wasn't wearing a badge. And he wore a white fanny pack around his waist, where he kept his pen and a small note pad. He was heavyset, kind of nerdy, really. He wore an old baseball cap and glasses with huge soda-bottle lenses."

"That's a great start. Could you come down to the station and work with our forensic artist?"

"Of course, but I don't think..."

"It's not your job to think."

Bad Cop Luke was back. "Have you always been such a jerk?" she snapped.

Luke ignored her remark and scratched his head.

"Okay, I wasn't going to tell you this. I can just see you flapping your loose lips to the press, but the killer pinned a white piece of paper to the blouses of each of the girls. The paper had a copy of the dead girls' signatures. Our killer left an actual signature behind."

"And you think that piece of paper might have been Xeroxed from the signatures the guy got from the pageant programs?" Flippy asked, gritting her teeth over the loose-lips remark.

"Has to have been. We've got to find that big flowered-shirt guy. Either he's the killer or he'll lead us to the killer."

"Luke, my name was on that program. I gave him my signature."

"Okay, now we know for sure you're on his list. I'm going to notify the chief, and we're going to take the proper precautions. Maybe I can start by protecting you from those men sleeping outside the office in your bushes."

"They're not *my* bushes, they belong to the city. Anyway, they're harmless."

"Homeless doesn't mean harmless. Your receptionist tells me you keep them supplied with doughnuts and coffee."

"Misty talks too much."

"I suppose you ask them what kind they like?"

"Glazed."

Luke rolled his eyes.

"If you don't stop feeding them, they're going to keep coming back, like cats."

"Don't be an idiot," Flippy said. "They're just camping out temporarily. They've simply hit a rough patch. They're unemployed and down on their luck. They have nowhere else to go. They're not bothering anybody."

"How do you know?"

"I asked them."

"You talk to them?"

"Yes, of course. They're not monsters. They're human beings."

"You're a soft touch, Flippy. I'm surprised you haven't offered to take them home with you. I'm going to have to insist you stop associating with the homeless people."

"Insist?"

"Strongly recommend."

"Why?"

"For the obvious reasons," Luke answered. "What if one of them is the killer disguised as a homeless man? What if he's biding his time, waiting right outside your door until you're alone, waiting for the right moment before he grabs his next victim? There's a very real possibility you could be in danger."

"Why do you even care?" Flippy inquired.

"I don't." Luke fidgeted with a photo on the desk and did his best to look aloof.

"Well, then let's drop this whole protection façade. And tell me why you're really here. It's not to babysit me or to protect me, as you claim. You're pumping me for information, information I don't have or don't remember."

"You let me be the judge of that."

"You don't even want me on this task force. You'd like the campus police to disappear. You don't even want to be here."

"I sure as hell don't want to be here babysitting a bubble-headed bimbo."

"Bimbo?"

"I'm not the one who goes to bars, gets hammered, and picks up the first guy she sees."

Flippy frowned. "Are we back on that tired horse again? I told you, you need to get over that."

"And I told *you* I'm already over it. I don't *need* you. You're all wrong for this assignment, and I'm going to tell the chief that."

"You don't think I have the brains to be on this task force, do you?" Flippy challenged.

"I never said that." Luke's belligerent stare said it all.

"Not in so many words. You called me a bimbo."

"You don't know what I'm thinking. Are you a mind reader now, like Crystal Ball Kate?"

"When it comes to you, yes. You're pathetically transparent."

Luke narrowed his eyes and pierced her with his steely gaze. "You don't have the sense you were born with. Take the homeless men. What you're doing is breaking the law. Did you know Graysville just passed an ordinance against homeless drifters? You're not allowed to feed them. No more soup kitchens or homeless shelters. We're trying to clean up Graysville. You could be fined."

"Then let them fine me. I think it's shameful that the city is trying to shut them down."

"You need to call the police about them," Luke smirked, in his best back-to-business voice.

"I thought *you* were the police. And I did call the police to see if there was some kind of homeless shelter that could take them in. You know what their advice was? Turn on the sprinkler system and hose them down. Even if I didn't deem it cruel and unusual punishment to douse a poor, unfortunate homeless person, the campus police department can't afford a sprinkler system. So I let them stay. Anyway, I like having them around. There's safety in numbers."

Luke examined her like she had a screw loose. He probably wouldn't understand that she found a measure of comfort in the presence of those homeless men who slept in the generous shade of the box hedges that lined the front of her office window. And now a growing number of them were making their home in various-sized cardboard boxes, jockeying for position and settling in for a long winter.

One man had told her he'd been drawn to the smell of the rosebushes outside her office, that the smell of roses reminded him of home.

"A couple of those guys are pretty scruffy looking," Luke said. "Have you seen the way they just walk up and down Main Street, wearing all the clothes they own on their backs? They carry all their possessions in large plastic black garbage bags, and they reek. Some of them probably haven't bathed in months."

"But the smell from DaVinci's kind of masks the scent." Flippy laughed, not wanting to admit to Luke that she was getting used to their odor.

"You mean the stench," Luke said. "When I got here, one of them was trying to sniff freon out of your air-conditioning unit."

"Why?"

"To get high, Miss Crisis Management, Homecoming Queen Runner-Up, who doesn't know what's going on right outside her own office."

"I know everything that's going on."

"You need to get a lock put on that valve," Luke argued, like he was talking to a recalcitrant child.

"I'll get Misty right on that. Breathing those fumes can't be good for them."

Luke shook his head and his face grew serious. "Look, there's a meeting of the parents of the victims down at the Graysville police station this afternoon. Chief Bradley would like you to go, to reassure the loved ones that we are doing everything possible to find the killer."

"Is it a press conference?"

"No press allowed. Just family. If there were media, do you think the chief would miss the opportunity to grab the spotlight away from the FBI?"

"Why does he need me, then?"

"Because you're one of them."

"One of them?"

"You know, a beauty queen."

"Not technically. I was a first runner-up last year."

"You know what I mean. You're beautiful. Their daughters were beautiful. They will relate to you."

"I don't think it works that way."

"Those girls are a different breed," Luke explained.

"They're just people," Flippy said. Luke wasn't the

only person who harbored that misconception about beauty pageant contestants.

"Beautiful people," Luke said stubbornly. "Like you."

"You think I'm beautiful?" She knew it wasn't an appropriate time to fish for compliments, in the middle of a murder investigation, but her bruised ego needed reassurance.

"Well, hell, you know you are," Luke said angrily. Then he closed up tighter than a clam. A second later he blurted out, "You're enjoying this, aren't you."

"Do I look like I'm having fun? Luke, we've got to find this guy. We have to do whatever it takes. I don't want one more girl to be sacrificed because maybe I missed something. What are we missing?"

"If we don't leave now, we're going to miss the meeting at the station. By the way, Crystal Ball Kate and her husband are going to be there."

Flippy's face lit up. "I can't wait to meet them. You know, you could learn something from them."

Luke sneered. "This case needs more than hocus pocus. We don't have time to play psychic games. They're just the flavor of the month. But hey, we don't have much else to go on. So maybe a little help from the cosmos isn't such a bad thing. It can't hurt." Luke gathered up the photos scattered around Flippy's desk and replaced them in the manila files before he grabbed Flippy's hand and led her out of her office.

"Misty, your boss will be down at the Graysville police station for the rest of the afternoon," Luke instructed. "You have a file drawer around here with a lock on it? I need you to lock up these photos and the files on Flippy's desk until we get back."

"You can't order my receptionist around," Flippy said, frowning.

"You can order me around anytime, Officer Slaughter," Misty remarked, tossing her blonde curls and gazing into Luke's eyes as she angled her body to give him the best view of what she had to offer.

"In fact, you can take me into custody any time you'd like," she continued, holding out her hands submissively in front of her and slipping a note into Luke's back hip pocket.

"Call me," she mouthed.

Flippy twisted her face in exasperation. How her receptionist managed to stuff that shapely body of hers into so little clothing was a mystery. And the blatant flirting? Totally inappropriate in the office. She was going to have to have a serious talk with Misty.

Luke straightened and made his best effort not to stare at Misty, but he couldn't help strutting out of the office like a peacock.

Men. They're all alike. They are all cheaters. Just like my father.

When she and Luke left the office, the homeless guys were fast asleep in the bushes, the blankets she had brought them wrapped around their frail bodies, empty beer bottles lined up around them, propped up like a protective glass army. They had been careful to avoid crushing the rosebushes.

"Jesus, Philippa. You've got to get rid of them."

"Ssh, they'll hear you," she cautioned.

"They're passed out," Luke said. "Dead to the world. Don't you know anything? Your bleeding heart is going to get you into trouble one day."

Chapter Five

Flippy knew she was in trouble when, earlier that day, she was summoned by her boss, Elizabeth Beckham, director of campus security, to her office at Tanner Hall. Waiting outside the director's office reminded Flippy of the day she had been tapped for the Homecoming Homicides Task Force.

Then, too, students were milling around, huddled in corners, holding on to each other. Talking in whispers. Talking about the missing girl. Flippy took a deep cleansing breath. This couldn't be good. She had never been summoned to the director's office before. Had she screwed up somehow? Was she going to get fired? She'd tried to operate under the radar, to keep her head down, but when she applied for a job with the Homecoming Homicides Task Force, she knew she was opening herself up for scrutiny. Defeated, Flippy had visions of going back home to Atlanta a failure. And having to listen to her parents tell her "I told you so" again. She knocked on the director's door.

"Come in." The director's gruff voice.

The director was an imposing, but attractive, African-American woman, her hair more salt than pepper, who didn't tolerate nonsense from anyone. Born in England, she had the most beautiful British accent. When she spoke you felt you were being addressed—or dressed down—by the Queen herself, and she was rumored to have balls like Patton and the sterling credentials of Sherlock Holmes Meets Scotland Yard.

What she was doing in this backwater college town was a great mystery. The university had probably paid boatloads of money to get her here, and now their investment was paying off, because she was someone you'd definitely want on your side in a crisis.

The director had picked up Flippy's resume, riffled through it, then looked straight at her.

"You have excellent grades, impeccable references, impressive internships. Tell me, Philippa, why do you want this job?"

"I'm a Public Relations major but I minored in Criminology. This job would allow me to utilize my skills in both areas."

"That's a pretty answer, an answer I'd expect from a beauty queen, but why do you *really* want this job?"

Flippy hesitated and stiffened her spine.

"I need this job," she blurted. "My rent is due at the end of the month, and I don't have the money to pay it."

"Can't your parents help you out?"

"I pay my own way. I paid for my education myself."

"I see," said the director.

But she didn't see. Not really.

"It says here you're from Atlanta. Why don't you go back there? Why are you staying in a small town like Graysville?"

Flippy could ask the director the same question, but it was hardly appropriate. The director was not on trial here.

That's a question her parents had asked her dozens

of times. Graysville was a great college town, but why would anyone consciously choose to stay there after they graduated?

"I don't, that is, I can't go back," Flippy said.

"Can't or won't?"

Flippy thought about telling the director her story. Her pathetic story. But she didn't want to air her family's dirty laundry in her boss's office. That wouldn't elicit much sympathy. No one felt sorry for a beauty queen who not only had the looks but all the other advantages in life. No one could see what was wrong with that idyllic scenario. In Flippy's mind, going home was tantamount to giving up.

"I didn't want to take any money from my parents," Flippy said.

The director's doubtful look indicated a realization there was more to the story, that it wasn't just about the money, but she had the grace to let it go as she ruffled through her papers again.

"It says here you were the university's homecoming queen last year."

"Well, I wasn't really the homecoming queen. I was the first runner-up, and when—" Flippy tried to swallow the big lump forming in her throat and hold back the Niagara Falls of tears threatening to spill over.

"As I recall, the homecoming queen was killed," the director said. "That was before I got here. It was actually the reason I was recruited. That case was never solved."

"No."

"But there was talk, there were rumors, that you might have been involved, since you were in line for the crown, is that right?"

Flippy was suddenly tired. Her shoulders sagged and the bluster seeped right out of her, like from a defective balloon. She should have known she would never get away from the cruel accusations, the snide remarks, the speculation, the headlines casting doubt on her innocence. The jokes about Philippa Tannenbaum, the Susan Lucci of beauty pageants, who'd finally found a way to win the crown.

Of course, she hadn't killed Melinda Crawford. Anyone who knew her knew that was utter nonsense. Melinda Crawford had been a first-class bitch who'd connived her way to the crown, spreading lies and stabbing the competition in the back on her way to the top, but Flippy hadn't hated her enough to kill her. She hadn't even wanted the crown. Her mother wanted the crown, and Flippy had suffered the indignity of every beauty pageant since grade school to please her mother.

It was ridiculous for anyone to even think she was capable of murder. She had the opportunity and the motive, but that's as far as it got. Luke Slaughter had been there, too, supposedly shepherding them through the homecoming parade and the crowning ceremony on the field at halftime during the homecoming game. Melinda had died on his watch. If anyone should be blamed, it should be him. She supposed he'd paid for his mistakes. He'd been busted down to giving out traffic tickets to students who parked illegally on campus, and after a couple of months his application with the city police department had come through and he'd taken the job as a city cop. Then somehow he'd wangled his way onto the Homecoming Homicides Task Force. He had been given another chance. Didn't she deserve one?

Okay, this director could take her job and shove it. Flippy rose to go. She had tried to make things right. She'd spent a year wearing a crown that didn't rightfully belong to her. She had even taken the job as homecoming pageant director in the next pageant to try to set things straight. To give back. She should have known people had long memories. Now this serial killer was on the loose, and all the rumors were swirling around in the universe. She'd wanted to remain in the background and now she *was* the story—again. Not the place for a PR person to be.

"Where are you going, Miss Tannenbaum?" Flippy hadn't realized she'd left her seat and was halfway to the door.

She turned to face the director, red-faced.

"If you think I had anything to do with—"

"Of course I don't. I know you didn't. The former director of the campus police was looking for a scapegoat because he couldn't do his job, and that's why they brought me in. I deal in facts, Miss Tannenbaum, not fiction."

Not exactly a glowing endorsement, but the director's support offered a glimmer of hope.

"All I want is a chance, a chance to do this job I know I can do, to...make things right."

"And I want to give you that chance, so take a seat and let's get on with the interview."

Flippy slipped back into her chair across from the director, submitting once again to her iron gaze. This woman could give Maggie Thatcher a run for her money.

They skirted over the train wreck of her paltry six days in law school while she was trying to find her way.

But from then on, the director gave Flippy every opportunity. She'd started out as the campus police Victim's Advocate, where she learned a lot about being the victim. And once the pageant contestants started turning up dead, she wanted on the high profile Homecoming Homicides Task Force being formed by the campus police, the city police, and the FBI.

It was her chance to redeem herself, to prove she could do the job, that she wasn't just some brainless beauty queen trading off her looks, that she had something more valuable than a pretty face to contribute. If the man who had killed Melinda was killing again, she wanted to be front and center in the effort to find him and put him away so he could never hurt anyone again.

"If I place you on the task force, you're going to get thrown right back into the fire. You know that, don't you?" the director had warned. "Another dead homecoming queen turns up and you are thrown into the mix—again. People will talk."

"I can handle that," Flippy assured her. And she would handle it. She'd have to face her demons, survive the glare of the spotlight on her own time, but if she could live through that trial by fire, if she could come out unblemished, she could finally live with herself. So far, so good, until she had received a second summons today.

A secretary ushered Flippy into Director Beckham's office.

"Sit down, Miss Tannenbaum, and stop looking so worried. Despite what you might have heard, I am not a vampire. I don't bite."

"No ma'am," said Flippy, digging into the skin

underneath her fingernails.

The director may not bite, but she was not about to let Flippy off the hook on task force business.

"What are people saying about the investigation and how it's going?"

Flippy hesitated. She could hardly tell the director the truth, that the media and people all over the country were wondering why the campus police department was in charge, and how they felt the police were impeding the investigation.

"Um, that we're making progress." Flippy could hardly meet the director's gaze.

The director raised her eyebrows in doubt.

"That's a PR answer if I ever heard one. How's that campus-turned-city cop Luke Slaughter doing?" It made Flippy think of the Country Mouse/City Mouse story she'd read as a child.

"What did he say about me?" Flippy demanded. She knew she sounded defensive, but she didn't trust Luke Slaughter, especially not now.

"This isn't kindergarten, Philippa. We're not playing He Said, She Said. We all have to play nice in the Serial Killer Sandbox. I want to know what the city is saying about the way we're handling the investigation. I know you and Luke Slaughter are close."

Flippy's eyes widened. What didn't this woman know about her personal life? Was their one-night stand documented in her personnel file?

"We're friends," Flippy objected. "*Were* friends." Flippy decided to tell the truth. She didn't have anything to lose at this point.

"Chief Bradley says the campus police department

is overstepping, that while the girls were dumped on campus, they were killed in the city, so it's their case."

"We have no proof of that."

"He wants us to step down. The FBI wants to take complete control of the case, and the City of Graysville says they want the lead in working with the FBI."

"And?"

"And Luke Slaughter says that a beauty queen has no business being on this case."

"I want my seat at the table," the director said. "You are my representative. You absolutely *do* belong on this task force. You were tailor-made for this task force for any number of reasons. I fought to get you on there and I'll fight to see that you stay. But you have to do your part. My ass is on the line and so is the university's reputation. No parent is ever going to send their daughter to this school again if we can't catch this killer. We've already had dozens of girls drop out this semester. I want to make sure you can handle this new assignment, Philippa, or do I need to bring in someone more seasoned? The FBI is making noises about bringing in some of their people to handle press relations."

"No!" Flippy protested. "I can handle it. I will handle it. No matter what that snake Luke Slaughter says."

"I'm not interested in what Luke Slaughter has to say. I am interested in solving this case before the university president has my job. If that happens, then your job will be in jeopardy. I don't intend to be his or anyone's sacrificial lamb. You need to get this clusterfuck under control. I'm going to give you one more week—one week to set things straight, to get this investigation back on track, to reign in the media vultures. If that means working with Luke Slaughter to get that accomplished, well, suck it up and do it."

"One week. Director, ma'am, I can do that."

"Talk to your *friend* Officer Slaughter and tell him to stop sabotaging our case. We're supposed to be working together. Do whatever you have to do to get through to him. Neutralize him. Sweet talk him. Sleep with him if you have to."

Flippy looked at the director and her mouth flew open. The woman had eyes in the back of her head, but maybe she was psychic, too. Or maybe she'd been having her employees followed, to bars and back to their bedrooms.

"You know I was kidding about that last part," the director said, eyebrows raised, offering a hint of a smile. "Just don't let Luke Slaughter know I think Chief Bradley is a conceited SOB who doesn't have the experience to run a case of this magnitude. He's out of his league. Cowboy thinks he can skate by on his good looks and pseudo country-boy charm. Sucker tried to pick me up when I first got to town. I set him straight. He says he was just a lonely widower in need of companionship. I think he's just horny. But we're stuck with him, with both of them. So make it work."

"I have Luke Slaughter under control," Flippy assured her boss with a confidence she didn't really feel.

"See that you do. I know I'm throwing you in at the deep end, but I am taking a chance on you. Don't let me down. That's all. Now about this parents' meeting. Are you up to that? Or do you want me to handle it?"

"I assure you, I'll be up to speed and ready to

handle it."

"I don't like this idea of dueling press conferences. Everyone's releasing conflicting statements, the FBI, the city, us, the families. And meanwhile, no one is solving this case. And that bozo Bradley just hired a psychic detective agency from Atlanta to consult on our case. I've never heard of anything so idiotic. He's obviously desperate if he has to resort to woo-woo tactics. I want you to find out what they're up to and report back to me."

"Of course," Flippy said.

For the past week, Flippy had boned up on the case. She was as ready as she'd ever be. If Luke Slaughter didn't get in her way.

Chapter Six

Flippy felt their pain before she even entered the room. It was a palpable sorrow, pulsing like an irregular heartbeat, coating the room like an eerie mist from the underworld.

She ventured a look inside. Relatives of the dead, missing, and living pageant contestants were gathered in the break room of the Graysville police station. It was standing room only. Just thinking about those girls made her already queasy stomach clench.

Steeling herself as she entered, she shook hands with Will Bradley, chief of the Graysville Police Department. When she did, she had to look up. The chief was tall and built like a Mack truck. The director was right. He was a handsome devil, and so was the handsome devil, in the persona of Luke Slaughter, who stayed close on her heels.

"Thanks for coming, Philippa, Luke," said the chief, who directed a cordon of city police officers to tighten protectively around the silent wall of mourners. Flippy wished someone had thought to order flowers to soften the atmosphere. Just a small tribute to show how much the department cared.

"Glad to be on board," Flippy replied.

Chief Bradley directed their attention to a couple standing a few feet away.

"Philippa Tannenbaum, Luke Slaughter, I'd like

you to meet Jack Hale and Crystal Ball Kate—I mean, Katherine Hale, Jack's wife. I'm sure you've read about them in the papers. They just formed the Crystal & Hale Psychic Detective Agency in Atlanta. The mayor has authorized me to bring them on board to consult with the task force."

Flippy offered her hand to Jack Hale, who greeted her warmly. Luke gave Jack a perfunctory handshake and inclined his head toward Katherine, saying, "Ma'am."

Flippy also turned to Katherine, who grasped her hand in both of hers. The famous psychic's eyes were a startling shade of violet, just like they were on television. But up close, they were even more arresting, and they met hers and locked in. Then she drew back and dropped Flippy's hand like she'd been scalded.

"What's wrong, sweetheart?" Jack asked his wife, who had paled and looked like she was going to faint.

"What do you see?" he demanded.

Katherine was staring at Flippy as if she could see straight through her.

"A fire," Katherine answered. "I see a fire. And she's there. We need to keep her close, Jack. She's in danger."

Chief Bradley interceded and turned to Katherine.

"What do you mean?"

"She's the key to your case, Chief Bradley. She's the one he wants."

"The killer wants Philippa?" Luke asked, shifting his stance and rubbing his chin.

"Yes." Katherine seemed very sure.

The chief looked like he didn't know what to make of this new development. Luke leaned down and whispered into Flippy's ear, "Mumbo jumbo, nothing to worry about."

"I learned the hard way never to discount my wife's feelings," Jack advised. "She made a believer out of me. And she's rarely wrong. I'd put a guard on Miss Tannenbaum 24/7 until we catch this monster."

"What does she have to do with this case?" Katherine asked.

"Philippa was first runner-up on the homecoming court last year when the homecoming queen was murdered," said the chief.

Katherine shuddered and focused her unwavering gaze on Flippy. "I see blood. A lot of blood. The man you're looking for is out there. He's close. He has access, and he wants you. And I'm afraid he'll…" Katherine looked at the chief. "You'd better protect her. He's not done killing. He's just getting started. He's getting off on it, and he won't stop until he has Philippa. She will lead you to him."

Chief Bradley turned to Luke. "You heard the lady. From now on, you're on her 24/7. When she breathes in, you breathe out. Y'all hearin' me?"

"But Chief Bradley," Luke protested. "Are you going to listen to a bunch of—"

Chief Bradley cut him off. "Do your job, Slaughter. Or you'll be out of one."

Luke frowned and turned to Katherine.

"All due respect, Ms. Hale. You just met Flippy, so how can you know anything about her? True, you two have a track record, but I'm having trouble believing you just had this vision and, all of a sudden, we have the key to our investigation? Things just don't work out that way. It takes methodical police work to solve a case."

The chief stepped in before Katherine could reply. "Slaughter, the mayor saw fit to hire a psychic detective agency, and we are not going to ignore their advice. How many cases have you solved in the past year?"

Luke's face colored.

"And don't you go doubtin' their abilities. My mama has the sixth sense, sure as I'm standin' here. You learn to listen. She predicted that my sainted wife would meet an untimely death. I should have protected her. I didn't do my job, and now she's gone. She was the light of my life. I'm not makin' that mistake twice."

"Maybe your mama can solve this case," Luke muttered under his breath.

"You have something to say, Officer Slaughter?"

"No, Chief." Luke stared at the concrete floor.

"Good, because I know you don't want to go back to handin' out parking tickets."

"No, sir, Chief, sir."

Flippy ventured a look at Luke and smothered a grin. Then she scanned the audience, which was growing restless.

Chief Bradley stepped up to the podium. First he introduced Jack and Katherine, and a hushed silence fell over the crowd. Their swift work on the Sydney Strangler case was legendary.

"I want to assure you that we are doin' everything we can to solve this case. Whatever means we have in this world or the next. We are going to bring this killer to justice. Don't y'all doubt that."

Flippy blew out a breath as the chief addressed the crowd and looked at her expectantly, stepping aside to clear a space at the lectern and motioning her forward.

Luke escorted her to the podium.

Before entering the break room at the station, Flippy had thumbed through the homecoming pageant booklet. Of course her eyes had gravitated toward pictures of the dead girls first. And then they lingered on the photo of one of the Tri Delt girls, the missing girl, Traci Farris, her Little Sister in the sorority. That hit hardest. And left the worst taste in her mouth. And it wasn't from the greasy doughnut she'd thrown up that morning. If she could just get back the day she made the chicken soup. She had forgiven Traci, at least in her own mind. Jack wasn't worth it. But Traci had gone missing before Flippy had had a chance to tell her she wasn't going to hold a grudge.

Flippy had looked at her own picture in the booklet, above her title, "Homecoming Pageant Director." Remembering it now, that picture had her looking a lot less frazzled than she felt at the moment. More in control. And in light of Crystal Ball Kate's latest premonition, less frightened.

Then she had skimmed the ads purchased by the families, sororities, and fraternities who had sponsored the ladies, many of whom were in the audience, she knew.

The ads had been the worst: Alpha Chi Omega supports our sister... The Ladies of Delta Zeta proudly support... Congratulations, we are so proud of you... Phi Mu is proud to sponsor our sister... You ladies look beautiful tonight. We wish you the best of luck and love you dearly.

Shaking off the memories, Flippy looked around the bleak room and turned to Luke. "There should be flowers," she whispered.

"You see, that's why we need you. You know exactly the right thing to do."

Luke turned and took his position, flanking his fellow officers.

In the crowd, Flippy saw the frantic faces of Traci's parents, whose eyes met hers in question. What was she doing here? Did she know something? More to the point, did she know where Traci was? Flippy looked away. But not before she had registered the helplessness in their eyes.

"I want to introduce Philippa Tannenbaum, who is consulting with us on this case now," began Chief Bradley. "Philippa, as you know, was the director of October's homecoming pageant. In fact, she was first runner-up for homecoming queen in the previous year's pageant and then became homecoming queen. She worked with all the girls during rehearsals. Many of you have already met Philippa. She is our crisis management expert. And she is Victim Services Advocate for the campus police department, which is partnering with us on this case. So feel free to come to her or to Jack and Katherine Hale with any questions, leads, concerns, anything whatsoever—"

"Is there anything new to report, Chief Bradley?" one father interrupted.

"Not at this time. But I will let you know as soon as we've heard anything."

"Have you found the missing girl?"

Chief Bradley cleared his throat.

"Not at this time. Traci Farris is still missing."

Chief Bradley was turning out to be the proverbial broken record—*No, no, we don't know*. And he was painting Flippy and the psychic detective agency as miracle workers. Saviors. Holding them out as the last hope for these distraught parents, brothers, sisters, and boyfriends, when Flippy knew she was anything but that.

The chief looked at her expectantly and stepped aside. "You're up," he whispered.

Clutching the makeshift podium, Flippy dug her nails into the battered wood and turned toward the sea of anguished faces. She saw the placards carrying the names of the dead and missing girls, saw the hands caressing cherished photos of the deceased. It was reminiscent of 9-11, only on a much smaller scale. But this time there were no gaping holes in the ground, only a festering crater in the hearts of these devastated people standing before her.

They were expecting something important from her. What could she possibly say to them? What could she possibly contribute that would comfort them? She wanted her words to have some meaning, but would mere words be enough?

Usually quick on her feet, Flippy hesitated for a minute and opened the homecoming pageant booklet with trembling fingers.

Adjusting the microphone, she called out their names clearly.

"Meredith Henning."

"Montana Rountree."

"Natasha Hemmingway."

She read the names until she finished the list of dead or missing girls. Tripping on Traci's name, she bowed her head respectfully, wrested her clenched hands from the wooden platform and clasped them together.

The room went quiet as the mourners soaked up the tribute.

"I know you want answers. I can't give you answers. But I *can* make you a promise. I think I speak for the University Campus Police and the City of Graysville Police Department and the entire Task Force when I say we won't rest until we've found the person who is responsible for these horrendous crimes. We won't rest until we've found Traci Farris, and we pledge to protect the girls you've entrusted to us for protection. They are in our care, and you are in our prayers."

Flippy gave them her office number and her cell phone number and told them to call any time, day or night, if they needed her or if they just wanted to talk, that she was always available to them and for them.

Suddenly she and the Hales were surrounded by families. The girls who were left whispered the names of the dead girls, tentatively, entreatingly, like a prayer, as if they were on sacred ground.

"Meredith is such a beautiful girl," said one mother, her voice breaking into a sob, speaking of her daughter in the present tense, as if she were just in the next room.

"I wish I had been here. I wish..." sighed Meredith's father.

There were undertones of anger, joined by a chorus of despair, then just quiet resignation. Everyone wanted to talk to Flippy and the Hales about their daughters, about the last time Flippy had seen them, about happier moments, personal memories. And she stayed for more than an hour, trying her best to answer their questions, until the last parent was gone and she was totally drained and her head refused to stop pounding.

She had said goodbye to the Hales, who urged her to be careful as they left with Chief Bradley for a private meeting to discuss and dissect the case. The room had cleared except for Luke, who was nodding his approval. Then he closed the distance between them and reached for her hand.

"You helped them, I think," Luke said. Flippy looked down at their joined hands, but he couldn't or wouldn't let hers go.

"Pinch me," Flippy said.

"What?"

"I want you to pinch me hard, Luke, hard enough so I can feel it."

"Flippy?" Luke sounded confused.

"Pinch me, Luke, please," Flippy insisted.

Luke brought his other hand to Flippy's elbow and squeezed her skin.

"Harder," she urged.

"Flip, I don't see how this will help."

"I need to feel their pain, really feel it. I'm alive and their daughters aren't. It's not fair, Luke. It's just not fair."

Flippy collapsed against Luke, and he gently cradled her in his strong arms, rubbing her back in a steady rhythm until she pulled herself together.

"I know how you feel," Luke spoke softly, blowing his warm breath against the side of her face. "I wanted to tell them we were on the trail, like a Canadian Mountie. I always wanted to be a Canadian Mountie."

Flippy pulled back.

"Really?"

"Scout's honor."

"Of course, you were a Boy Scout."

"An Eagle Scout, as a matter of fact."

"Dudley Do-Right. Only Snidely Whiplash wasn't a serial killer."

Luke scanned Flippy's face. "You look beat, totally drained," he observed. "Let's get you something to eat."

"I'm really not hungry."

"Did you even eat lunch? You look wiped out. You need to put something in your stomach."

"I'm not hungry," Flippy repeated. "How can you eat after something like this?"

"Life goes on," Luke said. "You have to keep your strength up. I hate to admit it, but I think there's something to what that psychic told you. I always thought you would be on the killer's target list, but what she said confirms my theory. Besides, you look like you can use a drink."

Did she have to remind him what had happened between them the last time she'd had too much to drink?

"Look, we have a big day ahead of us tomorrow," Luke said. "I want to take you around to all the places where they found the bodies. But now we're officially off the clock. Let's go. The chief said to tell you how much he appreciates what you did for the families."

"I didn't do anything, really. I had no answers."

"But you let them talk and grieve. What you did was important," Luke insisted.

"I'm glad. I think it helped the families to see the Hales here. They're putting a lot of faith in Crystal Ball Kate."

"I'm going to reserve judgment," said Luke. "I'm a

believer in old-fashioned police work. But if it gives the families hope, then I don't see how it can hurt."

It was starting to rain, so Luke opened an umbrella and held it over Flippy's head until he managed to maneuver her into the passenger seat of his sporty red BMW.

"Nice car," Flippy said, veering away from the subject of the murders.

"It gets me from Point A to Point B."

"Where exactly is Point B?" she asked.

"How about The Zone?"

"That sounds nice."

"They have great gorgonzola burgers with Vidalia onions," Luke offered, "unless you're one of those vegetarians or vegans. You're not, are you?"

Flippy was actually starving, but the thought of eating a hamburger in the middle of a messy murder case made her stomach turn.

"I guess I could go for a salad."

"Rabbit food." Luke laughed. "You're a cheap date, anyway."

"This is not a date," she insisted, as Luke pulled into a parking space right in front of The Zone.

"Suit yourself. I'm still paying for your meal. It's on the department. The chief said I could expense it. And besides, my mother taught me manners. The guy always pays."

"That's old-fashioned." Jack had never had a problem with letting her pay.

"What can I say? I'm an old-fashioned guy."

The Zone was alive with students, and Flippy felt like they were all staring at her. Like they all knew about her recent breakup with Jack. Luke led her to a booth and signaled the server.

"Hey, Cathy, I'll have my usual, and whatever you have on tap, and Twiggy here will have some kind of salad. Flip—, I mean, Philippa?"

"The Caesar salad, please, and hold the croutons."

"Jeesh. You have to have something else to eat. You eat fries, don't you? Bring the lady a large order of fries, and don't skimp on the grease," he said, without waiting to hear her answer. "It's dinnertime, for heaven's sake."

"I don't eat fries. And I already had a big, greasy piece of pizza this afternoon."

"Not eating fries is un-American. Then I'll eat them."

"You look familiar," Cathy said, staring at her. "Weren't you almost the NFU homecoming queen?"

Flippy sighed. Did she have a sign posted on her face that read, "Loser"?

"I was the first runner-up."

"Homecoming queen by default," Luke added.

"You're Jack Armstrong's girlfriend."

Just keep it up, Chatty Cathy.

"Ex-girlfriend," Luke interjected.

"Ex-fiancée," Flippy corrected.

"Boy, you're moving up in the world, Luke," Cathy marveled as she sashayed into the kitchen, half her ass on display in her tight black hot pants.

"You must come here a lot, if you know the server by name."

"Sure. We all do. Actually, this is a big cop hangout. They have big-screen TVs. You can watch sports, have a beer, take a load off. They don't rush you. Food's good, too. It's a great place."

"Jack used to come here a lot."

"I wasn't going to mention he who shall remain nameless, but since you brought him up, I had to drag your ex in for drunk and disorderly more times than I can count."

"My Jack?"

"I thought it was over between the two of you."

"Oh. Yeah. Force of habit, I guess. He was drunk?"

"Force of habit," Luke answered. "The guy stays drunk. I'm surprised you didn't know. He had to sleep it off in a cell. It wasn't the first time. It won't be the last, is my guess. He couldn't walk on his own. His friends practically had to carry him into the bar. He's headed down the path of destruction."

Flippy took a deep breath and leaned back in the booth. Jack had been making noises about wanting the two of them to get back together. He had actually called her the other night, crying in his beer, apparently literally, asking her to take him back. Most likely from The Zone. As if she would ever go back to him! But, glutton for punishment that she was, she just had to ask.

"Was he, um, alone? I mean—"

"I know what you mean. You want to know if he was with a girl? Yeah, you could say that. She wasn't his usual type, though."

"Was she—you know?"

"Built? *Au contraire*. She was skinny."

Jack's usual type.

"Had a face like a horse, too. But he was too far gone to notice. She must have been some kind of sports groupie, or maybe an athlete. It's a hell of a thing, too. The guy had everything going for him. Big-time football player. Headed for the big leagues. Dating the best-looking girl on campus. That would be you. He had it made, and he's blowing it all to hell."

"It's his knee," Flippy explained, as the server delivered Luke's beer and placed a glass of water on a coaster to the right of the plate she set in front of Flippy.

"It's always something with these sports heroes. Everything has to go exactly their way. They can't cope with a bump in the road."

"A torn ACL is more than a bump in the road, Luke. It's going to take him a minimum of six months to recover."

"It's a tough break, but it's not a career-ending injury anymore," Luke pointed out. "His chances of playing again are eighty-five percent. And it's been way more than six months. He's still on crutches. The way I hear it, he's not even keeping his physical therapy appointments."

"How do you know that?"

"People talk."

"He knows he'll never be a hundred percent, and he's lost his chance in the pros, at least for the foreseeable future. Football was his life."

That about summed up Jack's priorities, even where she was concerned, Flippy thought, pulling the paper off the straw and pulling her water glass closer.

"You need something stronger than that. What will you have?"

"I'm not a big drinker," she started, then colored as she remembered that night a week ago. "I'll have an amaretto sour."

"That's a girly drink."

"Last time I checked, I was a girl." Flippy actually

managed a smile.

Luke threw up his hands. "Fine. Cathy, bring the lady an amaretto sour on the rocks."

"Will do, Tiger," she called out as she walked away to turn in the order.

"Tiger?" Flippy raised her eyebrows.

"What can I say? Some women find me ferocious." Luke hesitated, adding, "Actually, she says that to all the guys who come here."

"Right."

"Do I look like a tiger to you?"

Flippy laughed, and then blushed. Luke didn't look tough on the outside, unless he was riled, but in bed she'd found him anything but tame.

Luke's cheeks reddened too as he remembered that night, and his dimples reappeared.

Flippy sat back and contemplated the planes and angles of Luke's face until Cathy brought over her amaretto sour. Luke's eyes were fixated on her lips as she savored the sweet drink and sipped it slowly.

Flippy toyed with her salad when it came, while Luke practically inhaled his burger.

"You've hardly touched your salad. You're just moving the lettuce leaves around. Want a bite of my burger before it's gone?"

Flippy eyed it hungrily.

Luke tore off a piece of his burger and handed it to Flippy, who savored it.

"Eat and enjoy," Luke said, tearing off another bite of burger. "Or are you one of those girls who just likes to watch other people eat?"

Bingo. When she was with Jack, as well as during her pageant days, she never used to eat sweets or starches. Jack liked his women slim, like Traci. He'd dragged her to the gym with him every day. When people began to complain that she was losing weight, Jack said her weight was just being redistributed to all the right places and she was developing muscle tone. But all that dedication went out the door when Jack did. Now Flippy would make up for lost time. For a former beauty queen, she didn't much care how she looked anymore or what she put in her stomach.

Maybe she was deliberately sabotaging herself, trying to fatten herself up so Jack wouldn't want her back. That's what her mother would think. Barbara was one of the legions of women who had fallen for Jack's rugged build and charm and his calculated line of bullshit. But enough about Jack.

After a lifetime of abstinence, staying thin for one beauty competition after another, for her mother and then for Jack, Flippy was used to going without. Suddenly, a part of her had the urge to bite into something hot and juicy. So she bit into the burger Luke offered. Luke picked up a fry and brought it to her mouth. She turned away. It seemed greedy to enjoy even a simple pleasure under the circumstances.

"You act like you're afraid of it. It's only a french fry."

"Which will go right to my hips."

"Lucky french fry."

"Stop it, Luke."

"Stop what?" Luke feigned ignorance.

"The sexual innuendoes. The only reason we're even here together is police business."

"Which brings me to the next order of business. Your place or mine?"

"Huh?"

"You heard me. And you heard the chief. I'm assigned to you. From now on we stick together like Super Glue. Bottom line, you don't go home alone until this bastard is caught."

"What are you saying?"

"You're a smart girl. You figure it out."

"You're crazy if you think you're going to use this case as an excuse to get into my pants."

"At the risk of sounding crude, I've already been in your pants. Not that I wouldn't like to repeat the experience, but this has nothing to do with sex and everything to do with a serial killer. I can either stay at your place or you can bunk with me. And I've seen your place."

"You're dreaming."

"I don't have time to dream. Look, I don't need this disruption in my life. You're a pain in my ass and I'd just as soon not have anything to do with you. But it's easier for me to keep you in line when you're in plain sight. I don't have time to go back and forth to your apartment chauffeuring you around. I have a big test tomorrow. I'm going to be up all night studying for it. Some of us are still going to law school."

"Bite me. I didn't want to go to law school."

"Oh, yes, you did. You just didn't want to stay there."

"Whatever. That has nothing to do with what you're proposing. I don't have room for you at my apartment. It's..."

"Like I said, I've been to your apartment," Luke repeated. "You might have been too sloshed to remember. But I remember it very well."

"Then you remember how small it was."

"Size isn't everything."

"Could you be a bigger jerk?"

"I'll swing by your place, we'll pick up whatever you need, and you'll stay with me."

"What if I refuse?"

"I have strict orders not to let you out of my sight. When I'm not around, someone else will be taking over. You won't see him, but he'll be there."

Furious, Flippy whipped out her cell phone and dialed the director's number. When she started to outline Luke's outrageous proposal, she had to shield her ears from the scathing barrage that bounced back over the radio waves. Luke looked like he was enjoying the one-sided conversation.

"But Director," Flippy argued. "But, I— But he— No, I'd rather not be locked up in protective custody… No, I still want to remain on the task force."

Luke laughed, exposing those damn dimples.

"For how long? Yes, ma'am. I understand." Flippy frowned and placed the phone back in her purse.

"You arranged this with the director behind my back?"

"Whatever it takes to do the job, ma'am," Luke drawled. "I'm here to serve and protect. Let's just say Queen Elizabeth and I came to an understanding where you're concerned."

Flippy pursed her lips and scowled. "What about my car?" she protested.

"We'll leave it at your office and I'll drop you off at work tomorrow."

"I don't even know where you live."

"But I do. It's a nice place. You'll be very

comfortable there."

"Where will I sleep?" Flippy asked warily.

"You can take the guest room."

"You have a guest room?"

"We could both sleep in my room. That would be my preference."

"Don't even think about it. There will be no hanky panky."

"Oooh, now you're really scaring me."

"Luke, is this really necessary?"

"Yes, I think you know the answer to that. You heard what Crystal Ball Kate said. Do you want to end up like Meredith, Montana, and Natasha, or Traci?"

Flippy bit her lip. No, she did not. While she tried hard not to show it, deep down she was scared to death, and Luke could probably see right through her. She knew there was a possibility she was a target, and Katherine had confirmed it, unwaveringly.

"I'm not going to let anything happen to you, Flip. End of story. You'll just have to live with it."

"You mean live with you."

"That's just stating the obvious. But it's only temporary, until..."

"Until we bring that bastard down," Flippy said, rubbing her hands over her eyes.

"You still have that headache?"

"A bear of a one," Flippy admitted.

"It's because you never eat. Now take the rest of my burger." Luke pushed his plate over to Flippy's side of the table. "We're not leaving here until you finish it and eat some more fries, too."

"You make a lot of demands." Flippy frowned but grabbed the burger and began eating.

"Did you ever notice how your eyes light up when other people eat, but you won't put a drop in your own mouth? You get pleasure out of seeing other people eat. You're like that witch in Hansel and Gretel, always trying to fatten everyone else up."

"Don't psychoanalyze me. It's a simple headache."

"I've got some aspirin at my apartment. I also give a great massage."

"If I stay with you, you have to keep your wandering hands to yourself."

Luke rolled his eyes.

"A Boy Scout always keeps his promises, right?" Flippy asked hopefully.

"Believe what you want to believe. Boy Scouts are also resourceful. And always prepared. But I promise to protect you."

"I already told you, I don't need you to protect me."

"It's out of my wandering hands. I have my orders." Luke looked at the bill and slapped down a fifty. Hot-Pants Cathy came out of nowhere and scooped it up. She looked at Luke expectantly, giving him a good view of her cleavage. She and Misty must have been separated at birth.

"Keep the change," Luke said, lapping up the attention.

"Thanks, babe."

"Babe?" Flippy said with a bite to her voice as she finished up the rest of Luke's burger and fries.

"You jealous?"

"Of her?"

"Hey, she's hot."

"How do you know?"

"You can just tell."

"If she wanted to follow through, you'd be hightailing it in the opposite direction."

"If it makes you feel better to think so, then go right ahead. I can handle Cathy."

"Like you handled me?"

"If we're going, let's get out of here." Luke bristled, grabbing Flippy's hand roughly as he steered her toward the door.

"And what's with the hand holding?"

"Just part of the service. We aim to please."

"Well, Dudley, I expect you to *do* the *right* thing."

Luke laughed and pushed the door open. It had stopped raining.

Luke unlocked the car door and practically lifted her inside.

"I'm not helpless."

"I never said you were. I'm shielding you with my body."

Flippy rolled her eyes and didn't acknowledge the sparks that flew between them. Sparks that were almost visible in the dark.

After they had driven the few blocks to Flippy's apartment, she started to get out of the car.

Luke grabbed her hand. The man wouldn't stop touching her.

"Wait, I'm going to go in and check it out first. You never know."

"It's a mess," Flippy warned him. "It's really tiny. I-I wasn't expecting company."

"You don't have to impress me. I'm not Jack. Everything doesn't have to be in its place. As a matter of fact, I'm the opposite of Jack. I'm not uptight, and I like my women with a little meat on their bones."

"I'm not one of your women. Let's get that straight right now."

"Fine. Just open the door."

"Fine," she snapped.

She took out her key, and Luke preceded her into the apartment and flipped on the light. It didn't take him long to determine there was no one in there.

"This place is a dump, Flippy."

"I don't need you to tell me that."

"It's not even safe. It ought to be condemned. Why are you living here?"

"I don't have a trust fund." Actually, that was a lie.

"Neither do I."

"Well you're spending your money as if you were. You left that server a twenty-dollar tip."

"I can afford to be generous. It's the department's money."

"I'm going to get some aspirin," Flippy said, walking into the kitchen, which was just off the living room, which was just off the bedroom, which was just off the bathroom. She reached for a glass, ran it underneath the tap, and set it on the laminate countertop. She swiped the aspirin bottle from the cabinet, untwisted the cap, and downed two pills. Stuffing the bottle in her purse, she started packing.

"I'm sorry," Luke said.

"For what?"

"For insulting your place."

"Don't you think I know it's a piece of crap? It happens to be all that I can afford at the moment."

"Don't you have heat?"

"I have heat. I don't always turn it on."

"Can't your parents help you out?"

"Of course they can. But I don't want their help. I don't even want them to know where I'm living. Let's just say my mother would not approve. I've just started this new job. It's going to take a while for me to get on my feet."

"I take it your parents don't approve of your involvement in this case. Am I right?"

"If my mother knew I was anywhere in the vicinity of the Homecoming Homicides case, she'd drag me back to Atlanta herself. My parents are just getting over the fact that I dropped out of law school and am working in a law enforcement office. In my mother's mind, girls and guns don't mix. Yada, yada, yada. 'Don't you want to settle down with a nice boy, preferably Jack Armstrong, get married, and have some babies, hopefully in that order?' "

"A barefoot and pregnant beauty queen?"

"Runner-up."

In such close quarters, with Luke looming over her in that cold apartment, she was beginning to mellow, no doubt because of the amaretto sour. Suddenly she felt flushed and her nipples betrayed her, standing erect under her paper thin ice blue sweater. Something wet and squishy was happening in her panties. Her hormones were acting up. Crap. She needed to get control of herself and her emotions.

Being in her apartment with this man was triggering memories, memories she thought she'd repressed. Now she was imagining herself barefoot and Luke overpowering her. She was hallucinating, remembering the last time she and Luke had been alone in this apartment. The way he was looking at her, she knew he was remembering it too, in a way that said he wanted it to happen again, and right now.

"It's freezing in here," Flippy said, rubbing her hands together, trying to break the spell.

"I can see that," Luke said, his eyes fixated on her breasts.

Here they were, back in her substandard apartment for the second time in one week.

"My lucky table," Luke quipped, his hand resting on the kitchen table, observing Flippy out of the corner of his eye to gauge her reaction.

"Stuff it, Slaughter," she said. "Just because you got lucky once..."

"If we're going to be absolutely precise..."

"You're really pushing it, Luke."

"Just going to reiterate that if you want to stage a repeat performance, I'm up for it."

If Flippy remembered correctly, Luke Slaughter was up for quite a bit the night they had spent together.

"I mean, if there are any other boyfriends, fiancés, enemies, bosses, mothers, anyone else you want to stick it to, I'm your man."

"All right. That's enough. One more infantile remark and you're going home alone. Do I make myself clear?"

"Crystal." For the next hour Luke worked quietly under Flippy's direction, bringing suitcases, boxes, books, and clothing to his car while she finished packing.

"You don't have many clothes, do you? I thought beauty queens had an outfit for every occasion."

"I gave most of my clothes away to the women's work release program. Those women needed the clothes more than I did."

The next thing she knew, Luke was stroking her shoulder.

"Soft touch," he whispered.

Luke was breathing heavily and his lips were moving, but she couldn't hear what he was saying. Maybe he was whispering her name. He looked like he was going to kiss her. She held her breath, closed her eyes and waited, wanting him to.

"We'd better get out of here," he scowled, before making a final inspection of the place. "Hey, what about this box here? Does this go too?"

Flippy swiped the shoebox out of his hands.

"What's in there?" Luke asked.

"Nothing."

Flippy turned away and cradled the box, wiping away a stream of tears with the corner of her sleeve.

"Flip? What's wrong?"

"It's stupid."

"It's not stupid. You're crying. Now tell me. What the hell is in that box?"

After a heavy sigh she whispered, "It's my Jack-in-a-box."

"Your what?"

"Jack-in-a-box. My memories of Jack. First corsage, Valentine's Day cards, anniversary cards, photos, his fraternity pin, engagement ring I haven't returned yet...stuff like that."

"I thought you were through with that jerk."

"I am, but it's hard to let go of some of it. We spent four years together. I thought we were—oh, never mind. You hate him."

"You should too. Leave the box here. There's no

Marilyn Baron

room for that jerk-in-a-box in our new place."

"It's not *our* place."

Flippy turned away, but she couldn't stop the tears from flowing, and she clung to the box like it was a life raft.

Luke pried the box out of her hands and placed it on the small living room end table before he gathered her into his arms.

"It's okay," he soothed. "It's okay to cry."

"I feel like such an idiot. I thought I had cried myself out."

Flippy leaned into Luke and turned her face into his shoulder. He smelled as good as he felt.

"It's not okay," she said. "I hated her. I wanted to kill her, both of them, but I didn't want her to die."

"Hated who? What are you talking about?"

"Traci Farris."

"The missing girl?"

"She was my Little Sister in the sorority. She's the one I caught Jack cheating with."

Luke had been rubbing her back and kissing the top of her head, but he pulled away.

"Jesus Christ, Flip. Why didn't you tell me?"

"I feel responsible. Maybe if I hadn't gone over there that night, she would still be alive. I feel so guilty."

"You saw Traci Farris? When?"

"The n-night she went missing."

"What the fuck, Flippy? What are you saying? That you were the last person to see Traci Farris before she disappeared?"

"Stop swearing at me."

"I'll be doing more than that if you don't come

96

clean. This is a homicide case. And you're withholding material information. First I find you standing over Melinda Crawford's dead body, and now I find out you were the last person to see a missing girl alive. What am I supposed to think? You've been playing me all along. Is that why you slept with me?"

"You're way off base. And I wasn't playing you," Flippy said faintly.

"You lied to me. You lied to a police officer. You hindered an investigation. What else aren't you telling me?"

"Nothing. I swear. Jack was—"

"I don't give a shit about Jack," Luke said, shaking her by her shoulders. "I want to hear about you. I want you to give me one good reason why I shouldn't haul your tight ass down to jail."

"Let go of me," Flippy said, shaking him off. "I'll tell you, all right?" Flippy looked up into Luke's eyes and began to tell the story of the last night she had seen Traci Farris alive.

When she finished, he exhaled and pointed a finger accusingly in her face. "You had motive and opportunity. If anyone else finds out about this, you're toast."

"That's why I didn't tell you. I know I didn't do anything, and Jack couldn't have done anything. But I know how this looks. And I know it's my fault."

Luke shook his head and blew out a breath.

"It's not your fault, okay? She was the one who betrayed you, not the other way around. But Jesus, if you had told us where she was sooner, we might have been able to find her, might still be able to find her."

"Are you going to turn me in?"

"I'd love to, believe me. The first thing I'm going to do is question your jackass of a boyfriend and find out what he's hiding."

"I loved both of them. I'll never understand. But I didn't want this."

"I know you didn't," Luke said quietly. He put his hands on her shoulders, and then he released her.

"Did you ever think the guy might have been after *you*? And that Traci just got in the way? That maybe he expected *you* to be at Jack's?"

Flippy bit her lip. "That never occurred to me."

"Look, we're going to get you home...um, to my condo, okay?" We can leave the rest of this stuff, pick it up later. You feeling better now?"

"I'll be fine. But what about Traci? We've got to find her, Luke, before—"

"I know. I'm going to call Jack and find out if he knows anything, saw anything, remembers anything from that night. He was probably too out of it to be any help to us. Have you talked to Jack since that night?"

"No, he's called, and one of his fraternity brothers brought him by. I didn't answer the door and I haven't returned his calls. He's probably sick with worry over Traci and guilty as hell about what he did to me."

"Well don't call him. I'll deal with Jack from now on. This whole situation stinks for everyone. We can take the box, Flip, if it will make you feel better."

"I don't want it," she sniffled stubbornly, turning her back on it.

Flippy picked up her overnight bag, grabbed her laptop and a worn herringbone wool coat, slid past Luke, and turned off the lights.

Luke picked up the shoebox anyway, rushed to

catch up, and ushered her out the door, down the steps, and into his car.

While Flippy got settled and slipped on her seatbelt, Luke turned on his ignition and reached for his ringing cell phone.

"Slaughter. When? Where? We'll be right there."

"Look, Luke, I'm a big girl. I can call Jack myself to get information."

"Jack can wait." Luke's face was pale. "They just found Traci Farris."

Chapter Seven

Luke was quiet on the drive to Major Peyton Stadium. Flippy didn't have much to say either. So many thoughts swirled around her head. Luke said they'd found Traci's body. Traci was really dead, although Flippy wouldn't accept that until she could see Traci's body for herself.

"Someone has to tell Jack," Flippy said, trying to make conversation.

"Would you leave that bastard out of this? Hasn't he done enough damage?"

Flippy sat back uncomfortably in the car. Luke was right. She needed to push Jack out of her mind and her life, and the sooner the better.

"It's all still too fresh," she said. "The wounds." And she knew she was talking about more than just Jack. She dreaded seeing Traci again.

Floodlights and lights from police cruisers surrounding the stadium saturated the darkness. Police radios punctuated the silence with their static-filled chatter, leaving no doubt this was a crime scene. Luke flashed his badge and led Flippy through the police barrier.

"Hey, no civilians allowed," one cop said, stepping into Flippy's path.

"She's with me," Luke said. "Let her through."

Flippy wanted to straighten out that cop, tell him

she was part of the official investigation task force and had every right to be there. She didn't need to trail in Luke's shadow. But she docilely followed Luke down the cement walkway and through the Gate 11 entrance. She was numb. When was the last time she had been there? It was the homecoming game. She had ushered the three homecoming court finalists through this same gate and down the elevator on their way out onto the field. She'd removed her sash and placed it around the new homecoming queen and handed over her crown. A crown Flippy hadn't deserved. Everyone watching in the stadium knew it, too. She hadn't earned the crown. She'd been the runner-up in the competition, but when Meredith had been murdered, Flippy received the crown simply because she was next in line, the last one standing. It was humiliating. The headlines, the snickering glances, the whispers. But she'd held her head high and somehow survived the year wearing that stupid crown anyway, just to please her mother.

After Jack was injured, she'd stopped attending the games. She hadn't been back to the stadium since. Well, once, for the rededication in Major Peyton's honor. She had wheeled Jack down the same runway and out onto the field, where he uttered a few words about his best friend and got so choked up he couldn't continue. Then she took him home, and he got so drunk he passed out. That was the routine of their life together after his accident.

She and Jack watched the games on TV for the remainder of the season. Mostly she watched and he muttered, eaten up with regret about not being able to play. And since Jack had been sidelined and Major Peyton had been killed, the team lost every one of their games and never made it to the SEC championship. She had loved Major too. She could understand why Jack felt so empty without his best friend. And now she'd lost *her* best friend. Not in a pileup on the interstate but to a brutal serial killer in a senseless death.

However she tried to ignore it, the stadium was home to her. For four years Flippy had watched Jack play, cheering him on from the stands. But she wasn't prepared for what she saw there today. The medical examiner had not yet reached the scene. Traci—Traci's body—it wasn't really Traci anymore—was lying there, face-up, smack in the middle of the field, right on the 50-yard line, where the killer had dumped it.

"Bastard," Luke breathed. "Thinks he's clever. Trying to send us some kind of message. Not very subtle."

Flippy drew in a breath and stopped while Luke circled the body. She felt as if she had been gut-punched. Her legs wouldn't carry her. She wanted to scream, but no sound came out.

"Flip, I don't think you should see this. You can wait in one of the patrol cars."

Too late. She gathered her strength and moved forward. Traci's body was splayed on the Astro Turf, decorated by a logo with the school colors.

Traci was wearing a yellow bloodstained dress with a white sash. The dress was out of style. It definitely didn't belong to Traci. It wasn't the last thing Traci had been wearing. Well, to be honest, Traci hadn't been wearing much of anything when Flippy had last seen her friend. But she knew Traci's wardrobe. She'd helped her friend shop for clothes.

Traci, beautiful Traci, white as a ghost, the left side

of her face burned, her eyes frozen in a frightened, vacant stare.

"H-how did she die, Luke?"

"We won't know till the ME arrives, but she looks pretty battered. She was beaten, bludgeoned, tortured for sure, from the looks of it. Bled out."

Flippy approached the body, then staggered back.

"Oh, my God."

"Look, you don't need to be here. I can handle this."

"I do have to be here. She was my friend." Flippy knelt down and reached for Traci's limp hand.

"Don't touch the body!" Luke shouted.

"I know that," Flippy said, but she'd wanted to. She wanted to tell Traci to wake up, that the nightmare was over, to hold Traci in her arms and rock her and tell her everything was all right. That she forgave her for everything. Traci wouldn't have deliberately sabotaged her relationship with Jack. She was sure Jack had initiated it, and who could resist the package that was Jack Armstrong. He had everything—looks, personality, money, but he didn't think with his brain. He had turned Traci's head.

She had probably tried to fight him off, but in the end maybe she fell in love with him. Everyone did. Even Flippy's father thought Jack was a great guy, probably because he recognized a kindred spirit in his future son-in-law. He definitely had her mother snowed. Jack was the Golden Boy. Whoever said cheaters never prosper didn't know her father. And they didn't know Jack.

"Flip, come look at this," Luke motioned. "It's the killer's signature. She has a note pinned right over her heart. It's a Xerox copy of what looks like her signature from the homecoming pageant booklet. He got her to sign her name over her picture and they pinned the copy to her chest. Can you tell if it's really in her handwriting?"

Flippy bent down. It was Traci's signature. No doubt about that. In fact, she had been with Traci when she signed the homecoming pageant booklet.

"It's legitimate," Flippy announced.

"We'll have to wait for the ME to autopsy the body and determine time of death, but it looks to me like the body is fresh."

"She's not a body, she's a person. Does there have to be an autopsy?"

"Sorry, but yes. That's the law. We can learn a lot from that."

The thought of what Traci had already been through, and then the indignity of being cut open more than she already was, and studied like a specimen, sickened Flippy.

Flippy stared into Traci's swollen face, then turned around and retched all over the field.

"Come on, I'm taking you home," Luke said, trying to pull her away from the body.

"It was that greasy hamburger and fries you made me eat," Flippy accused.

Luke looked into her eyes.

"Flip. It wasn't the burger or the fries."

"Who's going to tell Traci's parents?" Flippy asked, allowing Luke to help her up.

"You're in no condition to—"

"I'm the one who needs to tell them," Flippy said. She strode over to the bleachers and sat down in midfield, directly across from where Traci rested. Luke followed her.

"When can they see her? They'll want to know."

"I see the ME pulling up. They'll transport the body to the morgue. This case will take top priority. Let me get you a time, and then you can call and have them come down and officially identify the b—, er, I mean, Traci. You can be there with them if you want."

"Yes. I want to be there."

Flippy squatted on the field, put her head down between her knees, and sucked in the cold air.

"Luke, can somebody cover her? She must be cold. She hates the cold."

Luke shook his head, hopped down from the bleachers, and said a few words to the ME, who covered Traci with a blue mohair blanket she retrieved from her car.

"I've got to call her parents now," Flippy insisted.

"Why don't you let them get her cleaned up, a little more presentable before you—"

Flippy had already pulled her cell phone from her purse. "Mrs. Farris. It's Flippy Tannenbaum. We have some news. Is Mr. Farris with you?"

"Have they found her?" Mrs. Farris asked, her voice strained. "Have they found my baby?"

Flippy was silent for a moment. "I'm sorry, yes. I'm with her now at Major Peyton Field."

"Is she...?"

"She's gone. I'm so sorry. We've lost her."

Flippy could hear the sobs over the line and then Mr. Farris' voice, resigned. "When can we see her? When can we see Traci?"

Flippy wanted to tell them that they wouldn't even

recognize her, that she wasn't really Traci anymore.

"Why don't you come down to the—um, morgue," Flippy stuttered. "I'll meet you there and then we'll go in together after they've, after she's ready for viewing."

"That's our little girl. Tell them to take care of our little girl until we get there. Will you tell them that, Flippy?"

"Of course. I'll stay with her. I promise."

She flipped off the phone and walked over to where Luke and the ME were standing.

"I want to go with her. I promised her parents I'd watch over her. Can I do that, Luke?"

"Sure. I'll be right there with you, if you want me."

"Yes, thank you. What about your test tomorrow?"

"Don't worry about that. I'll try to get in a few hours of studying after we get home."

Luke's eyes were on Flippy as she watched Traci's body being lifted up on a gurney and into the van. Then they trailed the ME's car as it drove to the morgue.

Flippy sighed.

"The guys are combing the area, looking for clues. They thought he might still be on the premises, but they've done a thorough search and they can't find him. Hopefully, we'll discover some evidence. He's managed to stay one step ahead of us. They've questioned a university custodian, but he said he didn't see anything. Jack and Kate are on their way to meet us, to study the body—I mean Traci—to see if she picks up any vibes."

"I hate this," Flippy said. "We should have had a guard out at the stadium. I knew this would be one of the dump sites. Okay, Luke, tomorrow we need to be proactive. We need to visit the other university landmarks. There's the chapel on the lake, the bat house, the new library, the museum, the "B" Dome. We need to make a list and we need to have those areas staked out. Crystal Ball Kate is right. He's not going to stop, is he?"

"No. He has no reason to. You can expect the media vultures to be surrounding the stadium tomorrow, doing their live feeds. That's what they are—bottom feeders."

"They're just doing their jobs." Flippy sighed again. "I'll brief them first thing in the morning. Could you put an officer with the Farrises? I don't want them hounded."

Luke delivered some instructions into his phone.

"Done." He turned to Philippa.

"You look beat, Flippy."

"I feel numb. I don't think I've really processed it yet. I can't believe she's gone."

"You had to have some idea. She's been missing for a week."

"Someone has to tell Jack. It should be me."

"I don't want you talking to the jerk. I'll let him know."

"The Farrises will want to take Traci back to Miami. But I can organize a memorial service here. Her friends will want to pay their respects. My sorority sisters will want to say goodbye. She had a lot of friends here, Luke."

"After we finish with the Farrises, let me take you home so you can get some rest. It's going to be a long day tomorrow. And Flippy, I'm going to find this bastard."

"*We're* going to find him," Flippy corrected.

Chapter Eight

It had started raining again, and Flippy was transfixed by the rhythm of the windshield blades and the eerie glow of the street lights as she and Luke rode down Main Street, heading away from campus.

Her cell phone buzzed in the darkness, and when she finally found it, in the maze of her overstuffed bag, and flipped it open, Jack's number was flashing. Again. Flippy frowned and didn't answer it.

"Who's calling?" Luke asked, keeping his eyes on the road.

"No one," she said.

"No one you want me to know about?"

"No one you need to be concerned about. It has nothing to do with the case."

"How do I know that if you don't tell me? If I'm going to protect you, you have to tell me everything."

"I don't have to tell you anything. And for the umpteenth time, I don't need your protection."

"How could you look at what was done to Traci Farris' body and believe that? That could have been you on that table in the morgue, Flippy. That's all I can think about. It could have been you. And Kate confirmed it again. She took one look at Traci's body and then she looked over at you and said, 'You're in his sights.' "

"I heard her," Flippy acknowledged.

"Did you, Flip? Then why aren't you listening?"

"I've agreed to go home with you, haven't I?"

"Reluctantly," Luke said.

Flippy was silent as the car rounded the curve into the Prairie Condominiums. The possibility that she was in danger hadn't escaped her. Luke entered a code at the gate. "I'll give you the code when we get inside."

"You live *here*?" Anyone who could afford to live in the Prairie Condos had to have big bucks. It was the nicest place in the city. "Are you a drug dealer or something?"

"You don't know everything about me."

"Apparently not. I thought you were a city beat cop and a starving law student."

"What gave you that idea?"

"The way you downed that burger at The Zone like you hadn't eaten in days."

"That's the way I always eat. I like to eat. You ought to try it sometime."

"How long have you lived here?"

"Since I was a freshman. My parents bought it as an investment. Next year, my younger brother plans to move in after he graduates high school. Didn't you mention you had a brother?"

"But mine is much older and more successful, according to my parents. At least until the bottom fell out of the market. But the patina remains. He's an investment banker in New York, and he has a perfect wife who works at a boutique hedge fund. They're the perfect couple with the perfect 2.5 children."

"2.5?"

"One on the way. *He* was planned." Flippy hadn't expected to tell Luke that. But she was in a strange mood. Seeing Traci on the ground at the stadium and again in the morgue had opened the floodgates of her emotions. She needed another drink, although she knew that wasn't the wisest idea, since she had been drinking the night she'd propositioned Luke, too. Had to have some fortification to screw over a friend.

"Meaning that you were, what?"

"An accident. You know. My dad is a serial cheater, and my mother finally caught him in the act. My parents were in the middle of a messy divorce, but then they decided to patch things up and, one make-up sex session later, lo and behold, I arrived on the scene."

"That's rough. How do you even know that's true, if you were in the womb at the time?"

"My mother tends to be brutally honest when it suits her, and, as it turns out, history repeated itself. Which is how my sister Natalie came to be."

"Bummer."

"It's a little more complicated than that, but that's me in a nutshell. Second child, always came in second, an unwanted by-product."

"I had you pegged differently. Daddy's little girl, leading a charmed life, can get any guy and anything she wants, trades on her looks."

"You're not wrong about some of it," I admitted. "Only Daddy had a lot of little girls. Maybe one day when I know you better, I'll tell you the whole story." Luke looked uncomfortable, like he didn't want to know the rest of that story. Smart man.

"Well, we're here," Luke said, pulling into a parking space and helping her out of the passenger side. "Home sweet home." He started to pick up Flippy's laptop, but she put her hand on his arm.

"You don't have to carry my books, Luke."

"It's all part of the service," he said, popping his trunk and lifting out her suitcase.

They walked up the steps to Apartment 5, and Luke disarmed the alarm.

"You have an alarm system?"

"You should get one for that dive where you live."

"Well, we can't all count on Mommy and Daddy."

"Mommy and Daddy don't pay for my alarm system, and for your information I'm paying them rent."

"They make their own son pay rent?"

"They don't *make* me pay rent. I believe in paying my own way." They had that in common.

Luke opened the front door into what Flippy could only describe as a showplace.

"Luke, this place is like Buckingham Palace!"

Luke smiled and looked pleased with himself.

Flippy ran from room to room, giddy from lack of sleep and the strain of the day, gawking like a star-struck kid. Which made no sense, since she had grown up with the finer things in life. But in the past four years she hadn't been around anything as nice as this. She didn't want to take money from her father. She didn't want anything from him. Unlike her mother, who had never worked a day in her life and was dependent on her husband for every dime. She was never going to be beholden to a man for money or support. Especially not a man who cheated on his wife.

Flippy could appreciate the gourmet kitchen with its stainless steel appliances, the hardwood floors throughout the apartment, except in the bedrooms and bathrooms, the gorgeous window treatments, the very serene decor. And, no clutter!

"Don't tell me you decorated this place."

"My mom did. Decorating is her hobby."

"Isn't she afraid you'll have some wild party and trash the place?"

"My mother knows me."

"You really are a Boy Scout."

"There are worse things to be."

Flippy wound her way into the living room and tested the couch and the matching loveseat for comfort. The room was like something out of a magazine, a masterpiece, adorned with Persian rugs, Oriental lamps and Venetian mirrors, not quite the Vintage College style to be found in most apartments in Graysville.

"I could get used to this."

"Do you want to see your room?"

"As long as I'm here, why not?"

Luke laughed and preceded her into a room off a long hallway.

"If I had known you could be impressed so easily, I would have brought you home a long time ago."

Flippy slapped his arm, but she couldn't stop gawking.

"Wow!" was all she could manage.

The cherrywood sleigh bed with a Delft-blue goose-down comforter looked inviting. She couldn't wait to dive into it. Floor-to-ceiling mauve Doupiani silk curtains shimmered on the windows. The plush wall-to-wall carpet was a cushiony cool gray-green in some kind of leafy pattern. And there was a bathroom en suite.

"Luke, are you sure this isn't the master suite?"

"You want to see my room?" He raised his

eyebrows.

"Only because I'm curious. I don't plan on spending any time there."

"Be my guest. He grabbed her by the hand and led her back out into the hall and then into a spacious master suite.

"What did I say about the hands?" Flippy stared at their joined hands.

Luke colored and dropped her hand.

"You're the touchy feely type," Flippy guessed.

"I get that from my mom's side of the family. If you ever met my mom, you'd find out in a hurry. She's a big hugger."

"What about your dad?"

"Definitely not. My dad is a clinical pathologist. He mostly hides away in his laboratory and does research. He deals with platelets, not people. In fact, he doesn't like patients. I don't think he's even seen a patient since his residency. And that's the way he likes it. He's not exactly cold, but he's pretty hands-off."

"I guess opposites attract, then."

"What about your parents?"

Flippy frowned. "My mother is in everybody's business and my father is more into monkey business."

Luke arched his eyebrows like he wanted to know more, but she wasn't about to spill her guts about her dysfunctional family.

Luke's room was decorated in muted blacks and silvers. It was tasteful and manly at the same time. His great big king bed loomed, and they both eyed it awkwardly. The sooner they got away from it the better. It was giving her ideas.

"Did your mom decorate this room too?" Flippy

asked.

"Yep."

"Your place is beautiful, Luke."

"Thanks. I really love living here. I hope you will too."

"You know this isn't a permanent arrangement," she cautioned. "Just until we catch the killer."

"That could take months."

Flippy shuddered. "Let's hope not. I'm not planning to stay that long."

"Who said I wanted you to?" The cool and sullen Luke was back. After a minute, he relented. "It's good to see you relax again. What you just went through was brutal, at the stadium, the morgue, with Traci's parents. I just want you to know I understand that."

"Thank you."

Luke went back out into the hall and grabbed some thick seafoam-green towels from a walk-in linen closet and pointed out that her bathroom was already stocked with soaps, a loofah, shampoo, and other "girly" bath products.

"It's like living in a hotel," she marveled.

"Mom wanted it to be comfortable. I guess she hoped that one day I'd bring a girl here and—"

"Give her some grandchildren? I guess all mothers are the same."

A scurrying sound emanated from Luke's bathroom, reminiscent of a large rat doing cartwheels. Suddenly, the whole house seemed to be shaking.

"What's that noise?"

"Oh, that's just Cruz."

"I didn't know you had a roommate. You locked him in the bathroom?"

"No. Cruz is my dog. Cruz Bustamante."

"Cruz, as in the former lieutenant governor of California?"

"Yes, but she answers to almost any name."

"He sounds like a Great Dane."

"Actually *she* thinks she's a German Shepherd, but in fact she is a very tiny but feisty Bichon Frise."

"What's she barking at?"

"The vacuum cleaner."

"Why?"

"She's afraid of the vacuum cleaner."

"Sounds like we have a lot in common. What is your vacuum cleaner doing in the bathroom?"

"I knew you were coming and I wanted the place to look decent. I didn't have time to put it away."

"It looks a lot more than decent," Flippy said, following Luke back into his bedroom. As he opened his bathroom door, a fluffy white ball tumbled out, yipping loudly in a demand to be lifted. Luke scooped her up into his arms and raised her over his head.

"Oh, you're precious," Flippy said, reaching for the dog as Luke transferred the warm, wiggly bundle into her arms. Flippy cozied up to Cruz and was rewarded by a series of face licks. Cruz was exactly what she needed now. The dog seemed to sense her distress. Flippy squeezed Cruz and drank in her smell.

"Don't let her hear you say that. She thinks she's an attack dog."

"Cruzy, woozy, you're awful cute. But she's such a girly dog. I didn't picture you with such a frou-frou pet."

"I love my dog," Luke said simply.

"Where does she sleep?"

"With me," Luke said, staring at the bed and daring her to reply. *In that big cozy-looking king-sized bed.*

Flippy laughed nervously and backed away from the elephant in the room.

"You should see my dining room table," Luke drawled.

Flippy's face flushed when she remembered what they'd done on her kitchen table a week earlier.

"Okay, enough talk about sex. I'm going into the living room to study," Luke announced. "I suggest you get some sleep while you can. You're obviously wiped out."

"I want to do some research on serial killers. See if I can get a fix on the guy."

"You don't have to stay up just because I'm up, but you can set up your computer on the kitchen table, if you'd like."

"Thanks. I think I will."

"Our man doesn't quite fit the pattern. He's a creative bastard," Luke said. "Let me know if you find anything interesting."

The last thing Flippy felt like doing was bathing in the stinking morass of serial-killer-dom. She'd rather be bathing in Luke's luxurious Jacuzzi tub, *with Luke*. But he was right. She was wrung out from the day. She ached for Traci's parents. She missed her best friend. She wanted to wash off the grit and memory of the crime scene, the agony of watching Traci's parents grieve, of seeing Traci laid out on the table before she was cut open, but she was too tired to shower and at the same time too wound up to sleep. She had a lot of ground to cover, so she kicked off her heels, stretched her toes, and eased into a pair of well-worn slippers retrieved from her overnight bag. She set her laptop on the kitchen table and turned it on.

The pitter-patter of Cruz's dainty footsteps echoed on the hardwood floor as she went to lap up water and then munch on the food in her stainless steel bowls. Once her tummy was happy, she nestled her doggy chin against Flippy's fuzzy slippers.

Flippy peeked into the living room, where Luke was stretched out on the couch reading a Godzilla-sized legal book and outlining notes on index cards. He looked tempting, sitting there. He really was a decent guy. Definitely not her usual type. Apparently she had always favored the big, brawny jock type for whom cheating came as easily as breathing. Almost married a guy just like dear old dad.

She gave herself a mental slap and dragged her eyes away from Luke and back to her computer. Any thoughts of Jack brought back thoughts of Traci, and she didn't want to go there right now.

After an hour at the computer, Flippy's neck bobbed and her eyelids drooped. She was falling asleep with her head in the baked beans, as her sister Natalie used to say. Cruz had fallen asleep on her instep and Flippy was afraid to move for fear of waking her, but her foot was growing numb.

Flippy couldn't concentrate, so she closed her computer and gently nudged Cruz off her foot. The dog rolled onto her back with her feet straight up in the air, and Flippy smiled.

Luke was still hard at work, so she tiptoed into the guest room. Too tired to even wash her face, she changed into Jack's old football jersey, her uniform as much as it had been his, and snuggled under the comforter. The pillow was soft and comfy and the satin sheets were cool against her skin. She didn't miss her rattrap of a room one bit. And, for the first time in a week, she was ready to slip out of consciousness with her last thoughts not of Jack and how much she missed him.

Flippy felt something pounce on her bed and a warm tongue lick her face. Her nose twitched. Jack? Luke?

"Cruz," she whispered. "Come here, girl. You can bunk with me tonight. I need you more than Luke does." Flippy grabbed the adorable fuzzball and snuck her under the covers where Luke couldn't find her. She was taking possession of the family pet.

"Who do you like best?"

Cruz answered with more face licking. She had always wanted a dog, but dear old mom didn't want dog hairs or worse on her valuable Aubussons. Now she had one, sort of, at least temporarily, for as long as she wanted to stay at Luke's condo.

She and Cruz settled in for the night and prepared to dream. What do dogs dream about? Flippy wondered.

A sliver of light shone in from the hall. Luke was checking up on her. Flippy pretended to be asleep. She pressed her face against the pillow.

"Cruz, are you in there? Cruz?" Luke stepped to the bed and pulled back the comforter.

"Cruz, you traitor. You just met her and you're already sleeping with her? What a horn dog!"

Flippy struggled not to smile and tried to mash her face further into the pillow.

"Number 10, Big Jack Armstrong." Luke was

obviously looking at her jersey, her threadbare jersey. He'd better not be looking at anything else, bare as she was under that jersey. She knew the jersey was riding up her butt. Damn. Luke had a perfect view.

Out of the corner of her eye she saw Luke pet Cruz under the covers. He dominated the room. His hand hovered over Flippy's head for what seemed like the longest minute of her life. Then he tucked back a lock of her hair behind her ears, and his fingers lingered there and traced a path lightly down her neck, causing her to shiver.

"You awake?" he whispered.

Flippy lay as still as a statue.

The back of his fingers skimmed her neck and traveled down the well-worn fabric, lifting it until his hand made a soft imprint on her back, pausing before he administered a gentle massage that slowly inched toward her side, at which point her body betrayed her and her nipples hardened.

"What did I tell you about those wandering hands?" Flippy whispered, in a voice raspy with sleep, trying not to jostle Cruz.

"Couldn't resist. You said you had a headache. I'm just giving you a massage."

Flippy shifted up in the bed and smoothed down her jersey. His hand fell away as she turned to face him.

"I said a headache, not a backache."

"I can't help it. I can't help remembering."

"That was a one-time thing," Flippy said, glad Luke couldn't see her blush in the darkness.

"Not technically," Luke answered, his voice rising.

"Shush. You'll wake Cruz."

"Cruz can sleep through an explosion."

She looked at Luke's face, bathed in the moonlight.

"My life is a train wreck, Luke. I'm not ready for any more complications."

"I'll take what I can get," Luke said.

"My best friend is dead."

"That's why I'm here. I knew you needed me."

Flippy's mind might not be ready, but her body was drowsy and vulnerable, her nipples taut and her breasts suddenly hungering to be stroked. She needed to feel alive. Her tongue was dying to taste Luke's lips again. And there were other parts of her body she wanted Luke to taste again, as well. A pool of liquid formed in her lower parts, parts that weren't wearing panties. If he didn't touch her again, and soon, she was going to disintegrate. She stretched her arms, dying to reach for him, wanting to lose herself in him.

"Flippy," Luke pleaded, his eyes going dark.

But somebody had to be the adult here. After all, this wasn't an X-rated slumber party. It was a murder investigation. She brought her knees up to her chest and wrapped herself in the bedsheet.

"I'm sorry, Luke. It's just not right, the right time, I mean."

Luke finally looked away from her. "Goodnight, girls," he sighed regretfully and slipped silently out of the room. He really was a Boy Scout.

Chapter Nine

"What are you doing here?" Flippy snarled as she walked into her reception area and found Luke sitting in her receptionist's chair.

"I'm relieving Misty," Luke replied innocently.

"More importantly, what are *you* doing here?" Luke bristled. I left you in bed. I mean sleeping. You were so exhausted I thought I'd let you sleep in. And how did you get here anyway? I was going to come back and pick you up after my test."

"I hitched a ride."

"You hitched? Are you crazy? There's a serial killer out there, and you hitched?"

"Don't lecture me. You were the one who suggested I leave my car here, Mr. Brilliant. You left to take your test, so how was I supposed to get to work?"

"I told you I was planning to pick you up. And I had you covered, don't worry."

"You had me covered? I didn't see anyone lurking about."

"That's why they call it *under* cover. You're not supposed to see them."

"Admit it, you don't have anyone watching me. Which is fine. I told you I don't need your protection."

"Calm down."

"And where's Misty?"

"She's working at DaVinci's."

"DaVinci's? But she works for me. What is she doing back there?"

"Apparently she and the owner are tight and he was short-handed, so she offered to work for a few hours."

Flippy sighed. Her talk with Misty was long overdue. The girl had a lot to learn about responsibility. This wasn't some part-time job. Maybe she was being too bitchy. Probably because she had a ton of things to attend to, and she had gotten a late start. And she was hungry. She hadn't eaten breakfast, and worse, she'd had no transportation to the doughnut shop, so the men living in front of her office were going to go hungry too.

"Did you take your exam?"

"I did. I'm just glad it's over."

"How do you think you did?"

"Hard to say. I didn't get enough studying time in, but you never know."

"You didn't have to do this. You're just babysitting me, and it's not necessary."

"I told you. You're stuck with me unless I have class, and then you get my replacement."

"How am I supposed to recognize your replacement?"

"You're not, if he's doing his job correctly. You got some messages," Luke said. "More than a dozen media calls."

"That was nice of you. But you shouldn't be spending time answering my phone and taking messages. I have an office to run and we have a case to solve."

"As I keep telling you, *you* don't have a case to solve. I do. And someone else called."

"Who?"

"Number 10, Big Jack."

"Not again. What did he want?"

"Has he been harassing you?" Laid Back Luke uncoiled, baring his fangs, and almost sprang out of Misty's seat.

"His prior messages say he wants me back. He apparently hasn't received the memo yet that I don't tolerate cheaters. He's confusing me with my mother."

Luke was not touching that subject with a ten-foot pole.

"I told him to stop calling you, and then I told him about Traci. He was going to hear it on the news anyway."

"How did he react?"

"He was genuinely upset. I told him I knew what he'd done, how he'd cheated on the best thing he ever had with his girl's best friend."

"Luke, you had no right to get into that with him. That's a private matter."

"The guy is eaten up with guilt, I'll give him that."

"What else did you tell him?"

"I told him to leave you alone and stop calling."

"And?"

"And that you were with me now."

Flippy sagged. "Luke, that's a lie."

"I know that, but he doesn't. You want him to stop harassing you, don't you? So I told him you'd moved on, with me."

"He's going to need someone. I'm sure he's torn up about Traci. First he lost Major, then me, and now he feels responsible somehow for Traci's death."

"He's not your problem now," Luke said. "Did you

123

find out anything in your research last night?"

Flippy sat on the end of Misty's desk.

"Just the basic run-of-the-mill stuff on serial killers. The first one I came across was Danny Rolling."

"The Gainesville Ripper."

"Yes, the guy who mutilated five students in Gainesville, Florida, in August 1990. And then there was Ted Bundy, who raped and murdered several young girls at a sorority house in Tallahassee. There was also a lot of information about the Virginia Tech shootings and the fatal shootings of the UNC and Auburn coeds in March 2008. But other than that, no leads. Then I fell asleep. But reading all that research about serial killers must have given me nightmares. Because when I woke up I had this sickening thought. What if it's not a he? What if the killer we're looking for is a she? Did you ever think of that, Luke?"

"It's probably not a woman," Luke said. "Female serial killers are rare. More often than not, they kill for money, and nothing major was stolen from these victims."

"Except their lives," she felt obliged to point out.

"But poison is a woman's typical weapon of choice," Luke said.

"Didn't we learn in criminology class that female serial killers may be more common than we know because they're pretty good at what they do? They're just harder to catch and they leave fewer clues."

"That's true, so we can't rule out that possibility," Luke agreed.

"Why would a woman do something like this?"

"Envy?" Luke suggested. "It would take a hell of a sick person, man or woman, to do what was done to those girls."

On that point they were in total agreement. Flippy shuddered just thinking about it.

Luke got up from the torn leather swivel chair, and his hands were making sympathetic forays in her direction.

"You know, no one is expecting you to solve this case," he said. "That's not your role here. A lot of us have been working a lot of hours, and we've come up with nothing. It's not all on your shoulders."

"Luke, my boss hired me to consult on this case. I am part of the team. Not to mention that this case is personal to me. I may not be expected to find the killer, but I'm committed to making a contribution."

"So am I. That's why it's so important for us to work together."

"Okay, well what's your suggestion, *partner*?"

Luke was obviously at a loss. Flippy was right. They were depending on her and on the psychic detective agency from Atlanta, and right now they had nothing.

"You're officially relieved of receptionist duty," she said. "I'll cover the phones. Now go over to DaVinci's and tell Misty if she wants to keep her job she'll get her scantily clad self back here, cover herself up, and cover this office. She *was* scantily clad, wasn't she?"

"I didn't notice," Luke said, but his dimples gave him away.

"Right. Now go over to DaVinci's and drag her back if you have to."

"Yes, boss. It would be a shame to give Misty the boot. I think she adds something to the décor."

"That's because she leaves nothing to the imagination and your brains are in your crotch."

"Then why did you hire her?"

"Maybe I saw something in her. Potential. She's tough. A little rough around the edges. But her heart is in the right place."

"And cheap?" Luke guessed.

"Probably in more ways than one." Flippy grimaced.

"Okay, I'm going, but I hate to leave you alone even for a minute. Are you sure you know what you're doing, cozying up to those homeless guys outside?" Luke asked.

"Yes, I'm sure. But I dropped the ball this morning. I had no way to get to the doughnut shop. Now they're probably hungry as well as homeless."

"They're fine. I just fed them on the way in."

"You what?"

"I dropped by the doughnut shop on the way over here for some doughnuts, glazed, as ordered."

"You d-did?" Flippy stammered, staring at Luke and maybe really seeing him for the first time. "Thank you. I really mean that." Luke was too good to be true.

"You're welcome. And since I know you probably didn't have breakfast, I left a couple of glazeds on a napkin on your sorry excuse for a desk."

"Well, I'm sorry my furniture is not up to your standards."

"Flippy, I think your desk is infested."

"It may be, but I don't care. It's my desk."

"If you don't eat those doughnuts soon, they're going to be carried away by the ants or the rats. I can give you some money to buy a new one."

"First of all, that desk is the property of the campus police. And I wouldn't take money from you. And if I had any extra money, I'd save it for a rainy day."

"A rainy day?"

"You know, for emergencies."

"Your desk qualifies as an emergency. This office qualifies as an emergency. And your apartment can't even be resuscitated."

"All right. Just say it. I'm a loser."

"You're not a loser. I didn't mean that. It's none of my business."

"Well you seem to stick your nose in my business on a regular basis."

"I'm just watching out for you. If you don't want the doughnuts, I'll eat them."

"Is food all you ever think of?"

"No," he answered, looking at her the way he had looked at his burger yesterday. "I actually have a lot on my mind. You want something from DaVinci's?"

"Too greasy," Flippy said, remembering what had happened to the remains of the slice she had force-fed herself the day before. But that wasn't going to stop her from scarfing down the doughnuts on her desk. When Luke wasn't watching.

"Oh, before I forget," Luke added. "There was one more message. Some ball buster named Barbara called. And she gave me the third degree. Who am I? Why am I answering your phone? Where is Philippa? Apparently she's spooked by these murders. Who the hell is Barbara?"

Flippy laughed. "My mother."

"Sorry, but she's a piece of work."

"You have no idea. Barbara elevates high

maintenance to an art form."

"You actually call your mother Barbara?"

"Yes, that way we can maintain the fantasy that I'm her sister. She has trouble acknowledging the fact that she has three grown children. But that doesn't stop her from being a snoopervisor."

"What's a snoopervisor?" Luke took the bait.

"She tries to micromanage every part of my life, pathetic as it is, and she has to know every intimate detail of my comings and goings."

Except when they were shopping. Barbara was the kind of mother who didn't subscribe to the philosophy of No Child Left Behind. When Flippy was growing up in Atlanta, her mother left her behind on a regular basis whenever they were in a shopping mall. She'd invariably lose track of her own daughter while she was busy racking up a national debt's worth of merchandise to spite that daughter's father. In Barbara's world, her husband's job was to make the money and her job was to spend it. And the sum total of Barbara's purchases reflected the number or intensity of affairs the man was having at the time. If he was being faithful to her, she'd pick up a sexy negligee from Intimacy to reward him. If he was cheating, she would charge up a storm at Tiffany's to punish him. Needless to say, Flippy and her mother spent a good deal of time at Tiffany's. Barbara was really good at her job, and shopping was really hard work, so she frequently lost track of Flippy.

She didn't want to be anything like her mother. About the only thing she had inherited from Barbara was her looks. She loved her mother. But she didn't know who she least wanted to talk to right now, Barbara or Jack. She decided to start with Barbara.

Flippy wandered into her office and picked up the phone, anxious to get the impending conversation over with. She didn't need any more complications in her life.

"Barbara? I had a message that you called."

"You can stop with the façade. I told you that you can call me Mom when there's no one around."

"Mom, then. What do you want?" Flippy knew she was being snotty, but sometimes she couldn't help herself.

"Who was that man who answered the telephone?"

"He's the new receptionist."

"A male receptionist?"

"Yes, he's nice to look at."

"What ever happened to that Missy person?"

"Her name is Misty," Flippy corrected. "She went out for pizza and she hasn't come back."

"So you're making enough money now to afford two receptionists?"

"No, Mom, we can barely afford Misty. The campus police are on a tight budget. She had to help out a friend, so Luke was sitting in for her."

"Who's Luke?"

"You remember, I told you about him. He was in my criminology classes, and we went to law school together."

I could feel my mother cringe at the mention of my short-lived law school career.

"You're not getting anywhere near that Homecoming Homicides case, are you? I hope you're keeping out of trouble."

"I'm okay, Mom."

She was sure her mother had visions of her

129

daughter fraternizing with criminals in her job with the campus police. And actually, she wasn't far off the mark.

"Have they caught that serial killer yet?" Barbara asked.

"No." She wasn't going to tell her mother she was now personally involved in trying to apprehend the serial killer, however peripherally, and that she might be his next target.

"I'm worried about you. I haven't even seen your new place since you moved out of the sorority house. I want to make sure you're living in a safe neighborhood, so I'm coming for a visit." She most definitely hadn't told her mother where she was living, no matter how many times she tried to pry her address out of her.

"I don't think that's such a good idea, Mom. I'm pretty busy right now."

"Too busy to see your own mother?"

Too busy to let her mother see where she lived and what she did for a living.

"Surprise. Your father has already booked my ticket. He's probably salivating because I'll be out of town for a whole weekend and he's contemplating all the mischief he's going to get into with his new honey while I'm gone."

"Mom, why do you put up with his behavior? It's demeaning."

"Because he's your father and, deep down, I know he really loves me."

"He has a funny way of showing it." His latest "honey" was Flippy's age. In fact, she had been a friend of hers.

"I want you to pick me up at that poor excuse of an

airport you have there. Third-world countries have better airports than Graysville. After we land, I'll take you and Jack out to a nice dinner."

"Mom, how many times have I told you Jack and I aren't together anymore."

"Well that's just because you won't forgive him for one little transgression."

"It's gone way beyond that."

"I'll bet he wants to get back together."

"He has been calling me, but—"

"You should listen to what he has to say, Philippa. He is such a handsome man."

Beauty's only skin deep, she wanted to say, but didn't. Barbara was all about looks.

"You're right, Mom. Jack is handsome, but he cheated on me. Behind my back, and in front of my eyes, with one of my sorority sisters. You may be able to live with that, but I can't. And, I may as well tell you, Traci Farris is dead. It's going to be all over the news today."

"Traci, that girl in the pageant, your Little Sister in the sorority?"

"Yes."

"I'm sorry, honey. Was it that serial killer?"

"Yes, it was."

"You see, that's another reason I'm coming. Someone needs to take care of you. I told your father that someone needed to watch out for you. I really think you should move back to Atlanta. Graysville is not a safe place."

"Mom, I have a job here. I'm not moving back, and I'm not running away. And I'm not the one who needs protecting. Who is watching out for you?"

"All men cheat," Barbara responded.

"No, Mom, I have to believe that some of them don't."

"It's such a shame that Jack had to get hurt."

"Yes, it is. But he threw all his eggs in one basket, and now he can't or won't do anything else with his life. He's been drinking, Mom."

"Then he needs you more than ever."

"He probably does. But if I take him back, he won't do anything to help himself. He's just depressed now, and he wants to bring me down with him. He doesn't really love me. Maybe he never did."

"You dated him for four years, Philippa. You were engaged. I thought you two were going to get married."

"Well, so did I, Mom. Imagine my surprise when I learned he couldn't keep his pants zipped."

"Philippa, don't be crude."

"Sorry, Mother."

"Do you want your *younger* sister to get married before you do?"

"If she's found someone she loves and she's ready to get married, why should I mind?"

Talking to her mother was exhausting. Barbara was under the impression that you had to have a man to validate you, and Flippy was trying to extricate herself from all manly ties. The good thing was that Barbara had the attention span of a gnat. She was already on to the next topic.

"Tell me more about Luke."

"Lucas is just a friend, Mother. You wouldn't like him."

"Why not?"

"He works at the city police department."

"He's a cop?"

"A part-time cop," Flippy said.

After enduring what could only be interpreted as her mother's moment of silent disapproval, she added, "But he's going to law school." Why did she feel the need to defend Luke to her mother?

"Oh?" At last, a glimmer of interest.

She thought she'd throw her mother a bone. She could be cruel sometimes.

"And we're sort of um, dating."

"You're dating your receptionist?"

"That's just temporary."

"I know what's happening, Philippa. You're trying to get over Jack. That's understandable. And you're settling for second best. Very well, then, I will take you and Luke out to dinner. I'm bringing you a housewarming present."

How about some money so I can afford to warm the house, Flippy thought.

"The real reason I'm calling is about your sister."

"What about Natalie?"

Natalie had always marched to the beat of a different drummer. She was the black sheep of the family, which worked out fine for Flippy. It generally kept her off Barbara's radar screen. Her brother Neil had followed in her father's footsteps. Barbara, a former Miss South Carolina, had tried her hardest to mold Flippy into her image. But her plan backfired and Flippy had turned out to be a big disappointment to her mother in almost every way. First runner-up was not Barbara's idea of a success story. Natalie was the wild card. But thanks to Natalie, Flippy wasn't the biggest screw-up in the Tannenbaum family.

"You'll never believe what she's doing to me," Barbara whined.

She had a sinking feeling her mother was going to tell her.

"She's engaged. She was going to wait until you and Jack got married, but since that's not going to happen..."

Flippy frowned. She was happy for her sister, of course. But miffed that her sister had felt she needed to spare her feelings and wait to get married because she was the younger sister. Well, now she probably figured she'd have too long to wait.

"You should be thrilled," Flippy said. "You'll finally get to plan the wedding of your dreams." Left unsaid was the fact that her mother had just had to cancel all of her wedding plans and lose a sizeable deposit since Flippy had called off her wedding to Jack.

"That's just it. You know Natalie and Hugh both have unusual ideas about life. They can't imagine spending money on a wedding when there are people around the world who are starving."

"Does she want to get married by a justice of the peace?"

"Not exactly. She and Hugh have looked at some locations for the wedding, and they've settled on one."

"There are some great venues in Atlanta," Flippy said, thinking especially of the one she and Jack had picked out for their wedding ceremony—the Atlanta Botanical Garden.

"They want to get married at a state park," Barbara said flatly.

"Are you kidding? Well, there are some great state parks." She'd never actually been to one. Her parents' idea of a vacation had been a country in Europe. Roughing it was not the Tannenbaums' style.

"It's called Hard Labor Creek State Park," Barbara said. "And the wedding is right around the corner. June 13th."

Flippy had to stop herself from laughing. She could just picture the invitations:

MR. and MRS. ANDREW TANNENBAUM
REQUEST THE HONOUR OF YOUR PRESENCE
AT THE MARRIAGE OF THEIR DAUGHTER
NATALIE BROOKE
TO
MR. HUGH ANTHONY DIXON
SATURDAY, THE THIRTEENTH OF JUNE
TWO THOUSAND AND FOURTEEN
AT FOUR O'CLOCK IN THE AFTERNOON
AT
HARD LABOR CREEK STATE PARK

Barbara must be horrified. It was priceless.

"Where is this park?" Flippy asked wickedly.

"It's in North Georgia. It's some kind of a Boy Scout camp, I think."

Oh, my God. Flippy was having trouble keeping it together. *Go Natalie. You finally stuck it to Mom.*

"Well, Mom, maybe it's a nice state park," she offered.

"I've seen it. They want to get married at a campsite."

"That sounds lovely. I'm sure it's a nice wooded setting. The name implies there must be a creek."

"It's a campground, Philippa. It has picnic shelters." She could feel her mother shudder over the telephone line.

"Well, you know, you could have it catered."

"She won't allow me to spend money on food. She says her friends are going to provide peanut-butter-and-jelly sandwiches for the reception."

This was getting better and better.

"There are communal bathrooms," Barbara added.

"Mom, is this a joke?"

"No, it most definitely is not. She's not budging. I thought after we talk this weekend you could call her and talk her out of it."

"Mom, this is between Natalie and Hugh. It's their wedding."

"I know, and Hugh is a wonderful boy. He's a great influence on your sister. I adore him. But instead of registering, they want guests to make a donation to a charity."

"Well, that's a nice sentiment. Hugh is a good person."

"And they want your father and me to take the money we would have spent on the wedding and donate it, too."

Silence.

"Mom, I know you're disappointed. I know how much this wedding must mean to you—I mean, since mine is off the table." Didn't her sister know that weddings are mostly for mothers?

"Philippa, I don't know why she hates me."

"This has nothing to do with you."

"She's always hated me. You both have."

"Mom, that's not true. I'm sure we can compromise."

"You haven't heard the worst. She doesn't want paper invitations. Save the trees and all that. They want to e-mail the invitations and have the guests send their RSVPs only by e-mail."

Now Natalie had gone too far. Flippy tried to salvage the situation.

"Is there a city near the park?"

"It's near Madison, Georgia."

"Well, there you go. Madison is a beautiful town. They have lovely bed-and-breakfasts and quaint little inns and fine restaurants. Maybe the guests could stay in Madison and you could turn this into a destination wedding. Doesn't that sound promising?"

"She wants the guests to stay at the campground and cook out for all the meals. I refuse to stay in a campground. I have to draw the line somewhere. I can't invite our friends to a campground. Your father agrees with me on this. And that's not all."

"There's more?" Flippy said, stifling a giggle.

"After the wedding they're joining World Teach and moving to American Samoa."

"I thought Hugh just got a job as a receptionist at a doctor's office."

"He did, but that was just to earn some extra money, and he quit after one day."

"Why?"

"They asked him to do some filing and the files were color coded."

"So?"

"Hugh is color blind."

"Oh," Flippy said, grinning.

"After the wedding, they're moving to some place called Pago Pago for a whole year, and I know I'll never see her again," Barbara complained.

Flippy had stopped being shocked at anything

Natalie did a long time ago and instead always tried to make lemonade out of lemons, a trick at which she was very accomplished by now.

"Mom, it's just a year."

"Did you hear what I just said, Philippa? *Pago Pago.* And they're not even going to stay in Pago Pago. They're going to be teaching in one of the out islands. Manu'a."

"Manure?" Flippy spit, trying to squelch a laugh.

"Manu'*a!*" Barbara corrected. "It takes eight hours to get there by boat. Probably a canoe. Natalie says that the leading cause of death in American Samoa is falling coconuts."

"She's just joking with you," Flippy said, snickering.

"No, I looked it up. It's true. My daughter is going to be killed by a falling coconut."

"But I'll bet the surfing is fantastic," Flippy offered.

"Philippa, stop trying to put a positive spin on the situation. There is no upside or bright side. There's nothing remotely salvageable about this. I'm in a crisis. Aren't you a crisis manager? I need your help."

"I'm a crisis manager, Mother, not a miracle worker. Why don't you get Dad to talk to them? He's pretty persuasive."

"Your father says if I stick my nose into their business I'm going to lose her."

Flippy could hear her mother's muffled sobs.

"All right, all right, Mom, er—Barbara, calm down. I'll talk to her. When is your flight arriving?"

"Tomorrow, at three in the afternoon." Barbara sniffled.

"I'll pick you up at the airport."

"I can't wait to see you," Barbara said wistfully, and she actually sounded like she meant it. "And I'm sorry to hear about your friend."

Flippy hung up the phone and started cursing.

"Damn." Right in the middle of the most important assignment of her career. The timing couldn't be worse. The last thing she needed intruding in her life right now was her mother.

Luke popped his head in.

"Everything okay in there?"

"Barbara is coming to Graysville. Tomorrow. What am I going to do?"

"That's great."

"You don't understand. She can't see where I'm living. She'll freak out."

"Well, you're not living there now, are you?"

She stared at Luke and brightened. The Boy Scout was right. She was currently living in a very respectable, actually, *the* most respectable place in the city. It was even up to Barbara's standards.

"You have a point there. Now all I have to do is move all the rest of my things into your place. She'll snoop, believe me. Sherlock Holmes is a piker compared to my mother. I can't just have one suitcase full of clothes. She has to really believe I live there."

"What are you going to tell her about me?"

"I sort of told her that we were, um, dating."

"Could prove interesting."

"Don't get any ideas."

"Too late," Luke said. "I've already got ideas in my head about you. Does she want to stay with us?"

"There *is* no us. And Barbara doesn't stay with

family. She prefers hotels. Even though there aren't any hotels worthy of her in this city, in her estimation. She'll have to settle. But she'll only be here for one weekend. We'll go out to dinner. You'll stay away from the condo as much as possible. And she definitely can't find out I'm involved in this serial killer case. She wasn't too keen on you being a cop, but she perked up when I told her you were going to law school."

"Are we engaged?"

"Absolutely not. Not yet, anyway. Look, we need to hustle if we're going to pick up the rest of my things. If we start now, we can pull this off before she gets here. I'll bring my car too, so we only have to make one trip."

"Oh, and by the way, Misty says she's sorry. She'll be right over," Luke reported as he answered his cell phone.

"Good. I need to go over some instructions with her for the service today. We need to hold it as soon as possible. Traci's parents are anxious to take her home."

"After that we've got to go," Luke said. "The vultures are already at the stadium, picking over the remains."

"The vultures?" Flippy wondered.

"The media. The chief says you've got to issue a statement. Then, before the service, we need to hit all the sites where the bodies were dumped. And you said you had some other ideas about future dump sites, so let's swing by those and take a look."

There was so much to do and so little time. She still hadn't called Jack. He'd want to be at the service for Traci. It would be awkward, but she'd have to see him there. She decided to call one of Jack's friends and see if he could pick Jack up and bring him back home. She made a quick call.

"Okay, let me just leave instructions for Misty, and I'll call her on my cell phone later. We're running out of time."

Chapter Ten

Miss Congeniality was running out of time. And the clock was ticking for Philippa Tannenbaum, too, only she didn't know it.

Rodney took a good hard look at the latest homecoming queen candidate tied to the table in his workroom. She was so beautiful. She hadn't come around yet. He hadn't had the heart to wake her up. Like Sleeping Beauty, she was waiting for her Prince Charming to wake her with a kiss.

Rodney bent down and brushed his scarred lips against the girl's soft, pliant ones.

"Time for your close-up," Rodney purred.

The girl startled and opened her eyes, realized she was restrained by ropes, and screamed.

"Hush, now, you'll wake the dead, darling. I don't look that bad, do I?"

The girl trembled and tried to struggle out of her bonds.

"Who are you?"

"Your worst nightmare, sugar."

Rodney touched her naked breast and she shuddered and screamed.

"Now," Rodney said, calmly, cruelly pinching her nipple. "If we're going to get along, you need to stop screaming. No one can hear you anyway. Not way out here at the End of the World."

Rodney held up a silver hand mirror to the girl's face.

"You're all made up, and my brother is going to get some beauty shots, and then we can start the pageant. Donny scares easily, so don't raise your voice, or I'll have to cut you." Rodney drew a jagged knife and held it up to the girl's face. "I don't want to have to ruin that pretty little face of yours, yet."

Miss Congeniality looked at him with vacant eyes and passed out. The drug hadn't worn off yet. And he was anxious to get started.

He hoped this one had more spirit than the last candidate. She had whimpered throughout the whole pageant. Very unprofessional. She was no fun at all. But practice makes perfect.

He administered the smelling salts, causing the girl to stir again.

Rodney struck a match and held it up to the left side of the girl's face.

She tried to turn, but Rodney grabbed her roughly by the neck to hold her in place.

"Please don't hurt me," she begged in a hoarse whisper.

Rodney ignored her pleas.

"Now, sugar, stay still. This will only hurt for a minute."

Chapter Eleven

Flippy and Luke spent most of the day making the rounds of the places where the murdered girls' bodies had been found, retracing the steps of a serial killer, trying to get into his mind. Crystal Ball Kate and Jack had already driven the route with Chief Bradley and were back at the precinct discussing their ideas.

Flippy and Luke sat in Luke's car outside the football stadium, studying a campus map, trying to determine where the killer would dump the next body. Once they crossed the body dump sites off their list, Luke's plan was to visit the potential drop sites.

"Where do you think he'll strike next?" Luke asked.

"What makes you think he will? Maybe he thinks we're closing in, and he won't want to take a chance on getting caught."

"Oh, he's not finished, not by a long shot. He's on a mission, and it's not something he can control. He's already killed six girls, he may even have one right now, and there are thirty girls on the list, plus you."

Flippy shuddered. "If I had to guess, maybe the B dome."

"But that place is a hive of activity," Luke said. "Remember, it's basketball season."

"But the place is cavernous, plenty of places to hide, you know, the body." Flippy couldn't believe she was talking like this, so nonchalantly, about girls she had known so well. "Or he could settle on a quiet place, like the chapel. Kids like to go there during the day, but it's a pretty spooky place at night. A guy could move around there without being noticed."

"The chief has guards posted at those places," Luke argued. "Let's drive around and see if we spot anything suspicious. Maybe he's been there scouting out the location. Or he could be scouting out his next victim. Do you still have the pageant booklet? Any feeling about who might be next?"

"Other than the girls on the homecoming court, who are already dead, I don't have a clue as to who would be next. Maybe Crystal Ball Kate can help us out with that one."

"Kate insists that you're going to be the next one," Luke said. "She hasn't changed her story since she got here."

"He's not going alphabetically. It makes sense for you to dedicate your resources to protecting all the pageant contestants. Whoever's keeping track of them is not exactly doing a bang-up job, are they? He's managed to snatch the girls right out from under us. If we know this psycho is on the loose and we know his targets, we should be able to stop him or catch him."

"Some of the girls live in sorority houses, they go to classes, they go to bars until all hours of the morning, to parties all over the city, stay with their boyfriends at night," Luke rationalized. "It's tough to keep them in sight 24/7. We can't lock down the sorority houses, although we'd like to. But we're doing our best. You know how large the university is.

"And we have a small police force," Luke added.

"But your department is helping, and we're getting some assistance from the county PD, and the FBI is providing additional resources. We've put bodyguards on all the girls. A number of the parents have taken their daughters out of school until this case is solved. That's helped. But as far as my chief is concerned, this is still a local case, and that's the way we're treating it. The FBI doesn't automatically have authority. They're only here in our jurisdiction by invitation, as a consultant. In serial crimes, the rule is that jurisdiction is based on where the crime occurred and sometimes the who or what. There's no evidence the killer crossed state lines. This bastard is clever. He knows that."

"The parents are clamoring for the FBI to take the lead in this case," Flippy noted. "If I were one of the parents, I would insist on it, too."

"We've asked for their help, but if this case doesn't get solved soon, before we lose another girl, we won't have a choice. Everything will be out of our hands. Chief Bradley doesn't want to admit he can't get the job done, and nobody wants to be told that another agency does it better. The chief wants *our* task force to solve this case. Nobody at the university or on the local level trusts the FBI. As soon as we called them in, the case turned into a media circus."

"News flash. It already was a media circus."

"This case has become personal," Luke explained. "Chief Bradley's older brother works for the FBI. Apparently the chief has something to prove, and he wants his people to bring in the killer."

"That's silly and stupid. Sounds like your chief just wants to be a hero, at the expense of more girls who could show up dead or missing."

"Maybe, but he doesn't like outsiders in his business," Luke said. "After the service, we can go back to your office and go through the file of interviews with contestants and family members. The answer's got to be somewhere in those transcripts, and we should definitely take a second look at the video of the program. Have you heard back from your contact about who produced the video?"

"I told Misty to be expecting a call and to relay that information to me on my cell."

Flippy looked out of the car window. "What *do* we know about this guy?" Flippy wondered.

"We don't know anything about him specifically, but do know something about serial killers in general. Serial killers often exhibit latent criminal tendencies in their early years by torturing animals, wetting their beds, and setting fires."

"When I get back to your place, I'm going to search the archives of the *Graysville Reporter*. I can cover a lot of ground that way. I'll look for stories about any reports of kids torturing animals, or starting fires, incidences of escalating antisocial behavior."

"Great idea. And I'm going to get someone down at the station to get me a list of anyone on the university payroll who might have access to our buildings. We might cross-reference your list with that one. I want to know how our guy managed to get into a locked stadium in the middle of the night."

"We're going to find him, Luke. I know we are. What specifically have Jack and Katherine come up with?"

"The chief says Katherine predicts a new body is going to turn up soon. Although that's a little vague.

New bodies have been turning up on a regular basis long before she got here. And…"

"And, what?"

Luke hesitated and shrugged his shoulders.

"Like I said, she's been getting visions about you. She insists you're still in danger."

"Well, you're with me twenty-four hours a day."

Luke turned to face her. "I don't want you to worry, Flip. He's going to have to go through me to get to you."

"That's comforting, but I wish no one else had to get hurt."

"So do I."

Lucas pulled up to the next landmark on their list. Graysville Prairie Preserve State Park.

"Gray's Prairie isn't actually on campus, but I think it definitely qualifies as an NFU landmark as well as a National Natural Landmark. A lot of the kids go out there to park, fraternities take their pledges on road trips, and so on. It's really popular with students. Jack and I used to go there and—"

"I don't want to hear any more about Jack and what you used to do to each other, okay?"

Flippy was silent. Luke was right. Her personal business shouldn't enter into this investigation. And she shouldn't even be thinking about Jack.

"This spot is pretty much isolated, so it would be easy to dump a body here," Luke said. "They've got alligators, birds, all kinds of wildlife. Someone might have seen something; one of the kids in a parked car might have noticed something suspicious. We'll double back here at night, but I wanted to see the place during the day. We can climb up that observation tower near the visitor center and get a panoramic view of the preserve from fifty feet up. Our guy would have done that already."

Flippy got out of the car, and she and Luke walked first in one direction, then back in another. The Prairie was much too big to traverse on foot—21,000 acres according to the brochure she had taken from the visitor's center. There were eight trails for hiking, bicycling, and horseback riding. There was a lake for fishing, too, with a boat ramp for canoes and boats, even campsites and a picnic pavilion. Plenty of places to get lost and blend in. The ground was as flat as you might imagine a prairie to be. You could easily bury a body there, say in a swamp, or in the sinkhole. The latest addition to the park was a 1,000-foot boardwalk that had been constructed from the edge of the Prairie to the County Sinkhole, but this killer wanted his grisly work out in the open for all the world to see. He'd get off on that.

"Flip, over here. We've got footprints." Luke followed the trail and stopped at a clearing.

"Look at this. Someone has made a bed of pine needles, a resting place, just about the right size for a body. Wonder if this is the work of our guy? I'm going to get a squad car out here, see if they can gather some evidence."

Luke made a call on his cell phone. "What's our next stop?"

"The North Florida University Bat House," Flippy said, scanning the list.

"You know, in all the years I've been around here, I've never been there," Luke admitted.

"It can creep you out, if you spend any time there

at night," Flippy admitted. "There are zillions of bats swooping around. Well, it just seems like zillions. This bat house actually houses more than 100,000 bats. I took an elective course on bats once. Ours is the largest occupied 'bat house' in North America, maybe even in the world. It's like something out of a vampire movie, seeing all these small woolly brown creatures flying like acrobats, arcing slowly across the sky."

"Is this it?" Luke asked when he pulled up to park and pointed at the structure. "It's just an open, free-standing hut?"

"Yes, the university and the University Athletic Association built it."

"It's the perfect size for a body. Our guy could hide in the trees over there and when the coast is clear, he could drag out the body and place it right under the roof of the bat house. And watch the bats cover the victim and suck her blood."

"They don't suck blood, silly, they eat insects. These are Brazilian Free-Tailed Bats and Southeastern Bats. Every night these bats eat ten to twenty million insects. Nursing mothers can eat up to 125 percent of their body weight in insects each night."

"Who needs pest control when you have your own bat force?"

"That's not a joke. That's exactly what they do."

"We need to post a man here. Our guy has probably cased this place. It's perfect for him. It's simple and symbolic, symmetrical. Fits our guy to a T." Luke made some notes. "The chief will want to hear about this."

"Where do we go next?" Flippy asked.

"Well, there's the museum, but it's locked at night.

It would be almost impossible for him to get in there."

"He got into the stadium, didn't he?"

"Well the museum probably has cameras, lots of security, but it may not be open enough for our killer," Luke said.

"And then there's the chapel overlooking the lake," Flippy added. "Another likely spot. Very romantic. That could appeal to a twisted mind."

"Nothing romantic about what this guy does to the girls," Luke muttered. "It's sick."

"But we have to get into the mind of the serial killer, Luke. He could find that location appealing for some reason."

"Let's do that tomorrow. I'm getting hungry. How about you?"

"You're always hungry, Luke. But I could go for something."

"Okay, why don't we swing back by your office? You can touch base with Misty, see if everything is lined up for the service, and then we can grab a bite at DaVinci's and still make it to the service in plenty of time."

"And you can get another look at Misty, if I'm hearing you correctly."

"I'm not interested in Misty. I mean not in the way you mean. I mean, what normal guy wouldn't be, but..."

"Which proves my point, that you're just a typical guy interested in only one thing."

"You're confusing me with Jack. I am not a cheater. If I had someone like you, I'd never look at another woman."

"I've heard that line before."

"If I said it, I would mean it, Scout's honor."

Flippy smiled. She was starting to believe that Luke meant what he said.

When they arrived at the office, Flippy noticed something was different, but she couldn't place the discrepancy. When she walked into her outer office, Misty confronted her.

"They've run them off," Misty said furiously.

"Run who off?" Flippy wondered.

"The homeless men. The police came earlier this morning and picked them up in a van and took them somewhere with all their bags and things, and now they're gone and I don't know where. I tried to stop them."

Flippy swerved on Luke.

"Do you know anything about this?" she accused.

Luke blushed. "I did call the office yesterday to complain about the men. I was only concerned for your safety."

"Luke, I asked you not to interfere. They were not hurting anyone, and now they could be out in the cold somewhere, hungry, helpless."

Luke looked helpless himself. "I'll call the office and see what I can find out. But I told you the city has an ordinance against them. They're not supposed to be here. You're not supposed to harbor them."

"For heaven's sake, they're not criminals, Luke."

"And you know that how? This city is running scared. The last thing the mayor wants is a bunch of homeless men wandering around unsupervised."

Flippy shook her head to transmit her displeasure to Luke. Then she and Misty went into Flippy's office to review the list of items for Traci's memorial service.

"I've contacted the Farrises, the clergyman, sent

out an all-campus e-blast inviting students to pay their respects. We should have enough seating. I've made arrangements for the media to be there. I'll have everything they'll need. We're going to have light refreshments."

"That's great, Misty. You're doing a wonderful job, and you're a big help to me. It sounds like everything is taken care of. Can you stay until I get back from the service?"

"Yes."

"Any other calls?"

"A Terrence Scott called and said he was going to pick up Jack Armstrong and bring him to the service. And Jack Armstrong called several times. Wanted to know if you'd be there. I hope it was okay that I told him yes. Also, I postponed a couple of your meetings because I knew you'd be busy."

"Thanks, Misty."

Hiring Misty was beginning to pay dividends. She was proving to be less ditzy and more of a real asset.

Flippy and Luke walked to DaVinci's and sat at the bar. Flippy had a salad and Luke had a large pepperoni pizza. He offered her a slice. She removed the pepperonis and ate the cheese pizza plain. It tasted good. She washed it down with an entire glass of diet soda.

"My treat," Luke said.

"You don't have to buy my lunch."

"I want to. You've had a rough couple of days, and it's no big deal."

"Thanks, Luke. I enjoyed it."

"It looks like you're getting your appetite back," said Luke, after she lifted another slice of pizza from his plate.

"I figure I'd better eat now. Who knows when we'll get to eat dinner?"

"We. I like the sound of that." Luke smiled.

"Well I'm still mad at you for displacing those poor homeless men. I actually felt safer with them here."

"I'm looking into it," Luke acknowledged, adding, "And I'm still steamed that you arranged for Jack to be at the service. That's the last place he should be."

"I thought it was the right thing to do. Jack needs some closure. We both do."

"Well, I hope you're not going to let him sweet talk you back into his bed."

"That will never happen. I promise you that."

After lunch, they walked to Luke's car and drove to the memorial service. The auditorium was packed, a tribute to Traci. Flippy and Luke had just started down the aisle to talk to Traci's parents when Flippy felt a tug on her arm and heard a familiar voice. Jack Armstrong's voice.

"Flip, honey, I've been trying to reach you. I need to talk to you." Jack glared at Luke, and added, "Alone."

Flippy stared down at Jack in his wheelchair. She hadn't known how she'd react when she saw him again, or how she'd feel. It hurt a little less to look at him today, but looking at him brought back reminders of the night she had walked in on the two of them—her fiancé and her best friend. Sometimes it felt like it was all a dream and Traci was still alive. But considering the fact that she was attending a memorial service for Traci, that was hardly possible.

"Jack, we'll talk later. I need to see if Traci's parents need anything, and then I have to deal with the media. If you want to hang around, I'll be available."

"Available? You're treating me like another one of your appointments. I love you, Flip. You used to be in love with me."

"You loved me so much you had to sleep with my best friend?" Flippy started to walk away. "This is the wrong time and place. Later."

"Flippy, I can explain, if you'll let me."

She shook her head and walked away. Luke caught up.

"I'm proud of you. You were real cool. That couldn't have been easy. And I will definitely be there when you two talk."

"I can talk to him alone, I don't need a bodyguard or a babysitter."

"I just thought that..."

They were approaching Traci's parents.

"Mr. and Mrs. Farris. Is there anything I can get for you?"

"We're okay. We're going to take Traci home today. Your Chief Bradley is giving us an escort to the airport."

Flippy looked around and saw that a large number of uniformed officers from both campus and city police forces were in attendance. She would have to remember to thank Chief Bradley for that show of respect.

The president of the university made the opening remarks, then introduced the dean of students. A member of the clergy read some passages, and there was a poetry reading. The Farrises were too distraught to do more than listen, and the tears flowed throughout the service. Flippy would have liked to talk at the service, but she too found herself in no condition to participate. She hadn't broken down yet, but she was coming close to it now. Mrs. Farris had invited her to the actual funeral, which would be held in Miami, and she was considering going. She had been at odds with Traci the last time they were together, but the words of prayer washed over her and cleansed her, and she truly forgave Traci. They had been so close once.

Ultimately, she blamed Jack, but he wouldn't have strayed if she'd given him everything he needed. Maybe she had been too busy, not nurturing or sympathetic enough. She had to share the blame. Luke handed her a handkerchief to wipe eyes she hadn't even realized were tearing.

"A Boy Scout is always prepared," he mouthed, as she wiped her eyes. She smiled her thanks.

One by one, students got up and placed flowers on the stage, girls from Traci's sorority, people Flippy knew and many she didn't. Traci's body was already being prepared for the flight home, so there was no casket. There was a police color guard. Everything was very low key.

When the memorial service was over, she led Mr. and Mrs. Farris out a side door to where Chief Bradley was waiting.

"Thank you, Flippy," said Mrs. Farris. "Thank you for everything. You were a good friend to Traci."

Flippy winced and hoped they never found out what had gone on between the two girls in what were probably the final moments of Traci's life before she was snatched.

She and Luke walked to his car. Then she saw

Jack's friend wheeling him toward her. She had forgotten all about Jack. She noticed he still wasn't using his crutches.

"Flippy, you said you'd wait."

Flippy frowned.

"Jack, I'm really busy now."

"I *need* to talk to you," Jack said urgently.

Luke hovered, and Flippy signaled it was okay to leave them alone.

"What do you want?" Flippy asked.

"You know what I want. I want you."

"A week ago you wanted Traci. I don't think you know what you want."

"You're still mad at me." It was a statement.

"What do you think? I walk in on my fiancé and my best friend in a very compromising situation, and I'm supposed to forgive and forget? I forgive Traci because I know she didn't initiate this. And, she's gone now. Being angry won't do anyone any good. But you, Jack, you know my history with my dad, how I feel about his cheating, and you know that's the one thing I won't put up with."

"I don't know what got into me, Flip. You were never around. I'm still not over Major's death, and then you bailed on me, and now Traci is dead. She was so sweet and caring. She said she loved me, Flip."

Flippy bit her lip. "And you encouraged her, didn't you? You loved the attention. She was my best friend, Jack. Do you even get the significance of that?"

"I said I was sorry. You'll never know how sorry. Do you think it was my fault, that she's dead?"

"You didn't kill her, did you?"

"You know I didn't. It's just that if she hadn't run

out just then, maybe she'd still be alive."

"I've thought of that too. I'm just as guilty. But neither of us is responsible. The killer is responsible, and I'm going to get him."

"Flippy, if there is any way you could find it in your heart to forgive me…"

"You broke my heart, Jack."

Jack took Flippy's left hand in his.

"You're not wearing my ring," Jack noticed.

"I still have it. I haven't had time to return it. I'll mail it to you." She removed her hand from his.

"I don't want it back. I want you to keep it, in case you change your mind."

"That's not going to happen."

"Are you really with him?" Jack asked, indicating Luke.

"I've moved in with him," Flippy said. She hadn't intended to give a false impression, but if her mother called Jack, he'd back up her story.

"After only a week?"

"I've known Luke for years."

"Have you slept with him?"

Flippy pursed her lips. "That's not your business anymore."

"Flippy, just give me another chance." Jack was crying now. She hadn't seen him cry since they buried Major. He looked so forlorn and vulnerable.

"Luke says he brought you in for drunk and disorderly. You've got to stop drinking, Jack. And you're not using your crutches. The doctor says you need to exercise or you'll never be back to a hundred percent."

"You still care about me then?"

"Of course I do, as a friend. But I'm not coming back to you." She turned to walk away.

"Flippy, don't," Jack pleaded, grabbing her hand. "I love you more than anything."

"I wish you well, Jack." She looked at Luke and back at Jack and suddenly she didn't want to be there anymore. She reached out her hand gratefully to Luke, and he was there in an instant.

"Come on, Philippa, let's get you home."

Chapter Twelve

Luke drove by Flippy's office, and they walked in to retrieve her messages and gather some files to take to his house.

"I don't see the guys," Flippy said.

"They'll be back tomorrow," Luke assured her. "They're being well treated."

"I don't feel like going out for dinner," Flippy said. "Can we eat in?"

"Fine with me. There's a great sushi place right around the corner from my condo. I'll pick up something."

Luke was smiling as he opened the passenger door for Flippy and then ran around to hop in and start the car.

"What's that smile all about?" Flippy asked, noting that his dimples were making an appearance.

"I'm just happy, I guess. I'm right where I want to be, with the person I want to be with. It's no fun eating alone. I'm enjoying the company."

"Just so you know it's not permanent."

"I know that." Luke took the wheel. "How did it feel, seeing Jack?"

"Surprisingly, I feel relieved. Happy that chapter of my life is over with. I think if I truly loved him it wouldn't feel this good."

Luke smiled broadly. "Then there's hope for me,

for us?"

"I didn't say that."

"You didn't have to. I don't give up easily. That's one thing you have to know about me."

"That's good to know, since you're on the trail of a serial killer."

"Can we not talk about Jack or the serial killer for a few hours?" Luke said. "Let's just have a nice dinner, with a nice bottle of wine, and try to relax."

"I don't think that's a good idea."

"Relaxing?"

"No, the bottle of wine."

"Don't trust yourself?"

"Don't trust you, yet." *Or myself.*

"You can. You will."

"We'll see."

"You might need some fortification. Your mother's coming tomorrow."

She'd completely forgotten about Barbara's visit.

"Maybe you're right. But I don't think there's enough wine in Graysville to help me prepare for that."

They pulled into Luke's complex, and he parked the car and walked up the steps next to her.

When they opened the door, Cruz was already waiting at the entryway.

"Cruz," she cried. "Cruz." She lifted the dog into her arms, buried her face into the dog's neck—and then lost it.

"Flippy, what's wrong?" Luke looked alarmed.

Flippy couldn't talk. She just cried and wiped her tears on Cruz's nubby coat.

"Here, sit on the couch. I'll get you a drink of water. Then I have to walk Cruz."

"Don't take Cruz," Flippy wailed. "I've lost everything. I loved Traci. I wish I had told her that before she died."

Luke sat down next to Flippy on the couch and handed over an agitated Cruz.

"I think you've held it in for the past two days and now it's all coming out. It's okay." Luke rubbed her neck gently. "But I really have to take Cruz out. She has great bladder control for a small dog, but it only lasts for so long."

Flippy reluctantly gave up the dog.

"What kind of sushi do you like? I'll go downstairs, walk the dog, then get our dinner. There's a bottle of white chilling in the fridge. You get into your PJs and those cute little fuzzy slippers of yours, and I'll take care of everything."

"Thank you," said Flippy. *Luke really is special, and I do enjoy being with him.*

She went into the guest room, pulled on her pajamas, a robe, and the fuzzy slippers, and stretched out on the couch to wait for Luke.

The next thing she knew he was nudging her awake.

"Hey, sleepyhead. Wake up. Dinner's ready."

She blinked and smiled. "Hey, you, you're a really good guy, you know that? You're really sweet."

"Have you been tapping the vino while I was gone?"

"No, I just get this way when I'm sleepy."

"You mean sexy?"

"No, I babble."

"Well, keep babbling."

Luke pulled her up from the couch and led her to

the table in the kitchen. He had poured her a glass of wine and set out the dinner on fine china plates with cloth napkins.

"Very fancy for a Boy Scout used to roughing it," Flippy said, smiling. "I'm impressed."

"Let's just get something in your stomach, along with a little wine. It'll help you sleep. Then we'll tackle the files tomorrow."

"No, Luke, tonight. We don't have a minute to waste."

"Whatever you say." They ate and looked across the table at each other. She sipped her wine and played footsie with Cruz under the table. From the smoldering look Luke was giving her, she guessed he wanted to play footsie with her.

"Flip," Luke said, "I just want to say how happy I am that you're here."

Flippy was on her second glass of wine.

"You already said that."

"I know, but it bears repeating. And may I also say you look terrific in those PJs."

"This robe is hideous."

"I think you'd look beautiful in a potato sack."

"Thanks."

"You were much prettier than last year's homecoming queen. You should have been queen."

"That's nice of you to say. I wish I had won on my own merit instead of coming by the title the way I did."

"From what I heard, Melinda Crawford played dirty."

Flippy shrugged. "Maybe she did, but that's all in the past."

Luke cleaned up the dinner dishes, and when he

left the kitchen he came to sit with Flippy on the couch, where she was reviewing some files.

Luke took the files from her and placed them on the coffee table.

"You feeling relaxed yet?"

"Yup."

"You're looped. It doesn't take much, does it?"

"Nope. I have a very low tolerance for alcohol."

"How's your tolerance for me?" Luke inquired, moving closer and putting his arm around Flippy's shoulder. "I just want to give you some advance warning. I'm going to kiss you now."

Flippy's mouth opened in surprise, and Luke moved in smoothly to capture her lips and her tongue.

"Mmm," he purred. "You taste like fruit."

Flippy looked up at him cautiously.

"It's the wine."

Luke moved his hand up slowly under her robe and undid two of the buttons in her pajamas, cupping her breast in the palm of his hand and teasing her nipple. When she didn't object, he unbuttoned the rest of the pajama top and angled his head in to taste one nipple, then the other. She made some half-hearted protestations that turned to satisfied sighs before she snuggled against him.

He was kissing her, now softly, then insistently, and she was responding. It was the wine, she knew, but it felt good and she didn't want him to stop. Apparently, he had no intentions of stopping.

"Philippa, you're so beautiful," Luke said, kissing her tenderly, while he removed her pajama top completely, then her pajama bottom, until all she was wearing were panties.

She felt loose and limber, and her only thought was Luke and what he was doing to her and what she wanted him to keep doing to her.

Cruz was barking.

"Get out of here," Luke shouted and scooted the dog away with his foot. "Get your own girlfriend."

Flippy laughed.

He was hard now, and his penis was pulsing against her.

"Can you hang on a minute, honey? I'm going to put Cruz in my room and get some protection."

"Mmm," Flippy said.

Luke was back in a flash.

"A Boy Scout has to be prepared," he repeated his motto—really his mantra.

Then he was kissing her again, her lips, her nipples, her breasts, and he removed the last barrier, her panties, and touched her until she was wet and wild with her need for him. After she climaxed he climbed on top of her and drove into her, holding her shoulders and looking into her eyes, which had glazed over.

"God, that felt good," Luke said as he slumped over her body.

"For me too."

"I never thought you'd, I mean that I'd get another chance to, I mean I'm so crazy about you I can hardly be around you without touching you. What I'm trying to say is—"

"Sssh," Flippy whispered, placing her fingers on his lips. "Don't say anything."

"But I have to get it out or I'll burst," Luke said.

"I thought that's what you just did," she laughed.

"Flip, you're killing me here."

"You were saying."

"What I wanted to say is that I love you, Philippa Tannenbaum. I've never felt about anyone the way I feel about you."

Flippy sat up. "We've only been together for a week."

"We've known each other for years. I've been in love with you for years. I've dreamed about this—us—forever."

Flippy sighed.

"I don't expect you to say it back. I just wanted you to hear it."

"It's nice to hear, if you mean it."

"Of course I mean it. I want to be with you in every way. You're all I think about. Was it okay?"

"It was more than okay. Couldn't you tell?"

"I mean…" Luke began.

"You want to know how you compare to Number Ten?"

"Yes."

"Very favorably," Flippy murmured.

"I mean, Jack Armstrong is practically a legend."

"In his own mind, maybe. It felt great, Luke. I mean that. You don't need to compare yourself with Jack. Jack was a very selfish lover. He only cared about satisfying himself. I hope you're nothing like him."

They lay there contentedly on the couch, kissing, snuggling, until Cruz demanded to be let out of the bedroom.

"I hate to break this up, but I guess I'd better get Cruz," Luke said. "She's getting jealous. And she might just have an accident on my carpet to prove her point."

Luke jumped up and strutted over to his bedroom

door to let Cruz out. Flippy covered herself with an afghan draped across the couch. She was comfortable in this place with this man. Maybe too comfortable.

"I guess we'd better start poring over these files," Flippy called out.

"Okay, I've got some more studying to do first. Do you mind getting a head start?"

"I want to do some Internet research first, anyway," Flippy said.

She put her pajamas and robe back on and opened her computer in the kitchen with Cruz nipping at her feet.

She typed in "fires in Graysville, Florida, mysterious, deaths," and then hit Search.

A lot of entries appeared, so she clicked on the most promising links. There had been a rash of mysterious fires in Graysville over the last few years, and she went back farther, up to ten years ago and then fifteen years and bookmarked the articles she wanted to study. Then she honed the search by entering beauty queens. Probably nothing would come up, but you never knew. She wouldn't tell Luke about this right away. She would check out the stories herself to see if they panned out before she got his hopes up. But his idea of cross-checking the names of personnel at the university, or even ex-university personnel, would be a good plan once they got that list.

Of all the prospects, one stood out, making the hairs on the back of Flippy's neck rise. Was she having a sixth sense moment, like Crystal Ball Kate?

There was a story in the *Graysville Reporter* about a former beauty queen, Gracie Willis, who was raising two small boys after her husband had deserted her. One night, the younger boy, Rodney, accidentally set the curtains of his mother's bedroom on fire. He rescued his mother, but not before the left side of her face was burned and her good looks lost forever. She placed that article on favorites. Her computer wasn't hooked up to a printer, but she would print it out on Luke's printer later.

The boy, Rodney, would be about thirty now. She needed to do a search on him, see what else she could find. See if he was still in Graysville around the time that Melinda Crawford was killed.

Rodney Willis. Could he be the one? Unlikely. But in cases like this you had to take the breaks where you found them.

You're smart, Rodney Willis, aren't you. Top of your class at Graysville High. Where did you go to college, or did you? And if you did, and my hunch is correct, where did you go wrong, so horribly wrong?

Flippy made a note to check if Rodney had applied to NFU and if he had been accepted or rejected. If rejected, he could be bitter toward the university. And the fact that his mother was a beauty queen was a nice tie-in.

There was a picture of fifteen-year old Rodney. Looked like he could have been good-looking at one time, but he had extensive burns across his face, so probably he had been an awkward teenager. She'd need to consult with Katherine to see if she got any warning signs when she looked at his picture.

It says he has an older brother who is mildly retarded and attended the Graysville Community Day School for special needs children. Was he working? No picture of the brother that she could find. The mother...what ever happened to the mother? It didn't say she was killed in the fire. If she was disfigured, then she couldn't work, she couldn't enter beauty contests, or model. *Then, Rodney, it would be up to you to support your mother and older brother.* Caring for a brother with special needs would have been very expensive.

Flippy's fingers raced across the keyboard. *What kind of job do you have now? Nothing that would require meeting the public, not with that face scarred the way it is. And the girls would steer clear of you. Is that why you hated beauty queens, or did it have something to do with your mother? What set you off? Maybe you read about the NFU homecoming pageant or went there yourself and it was the trigger that dredged up your hostile feelings. Did you see an opportunity for retribution against beautiful girls, or the university, or both? Or am I just grasping at straws, practicing amateur psychology? I may need Katherine's help to analyze Rodney as a potential candidate.*

Why can't I find out more about you, Rodney Willis? There was a lot about Gracie. She was a beautiful woman. Won a slew of beauty contests in and around Graysville over the years.

Flippy copied down the last known address for Rodney Willis. Did he still live there? She was going to pay a visit to Mr. Rodney Willis and find out what he knew. She definitely wasn't going to tell Luke. He'd never let her go alone. But he'd certainly thank her if she came up with anything they could use. It was a long shot, but worth a try.

And what do you do with the girls once you get

them? We know you hold them for a week. Do you kill them in the privacy of your own home? Where do you do it? In a workshop? A basement? Or do you bring them to an off-site warehouse?

You'd have to be a strong man to lift the bodies, drag one up the steps of Centennial Tower, drop it over the side—unless you had help.

Look at her. She was silly to think that she had it right on the first try. It wasn't even worth mentioning to Luke.

"Luke," Flippy called. "Do you have a printer I can send something to?

"Did you get a hit?" Luke asked.

"It's probably nothing. I just want to print something out for future reference, maybe fax it to Katherine for her take." Luke came into the kitchen in his pajama bottoms and nothing else and hooked up his printer. She stared at his broad shoulders and his naked chest. She needed to stop thinking about sex and start focusing on serial killers.

While Luke went back to studying, she printed out the articles, folded them, and tucked them into her purse. Then she faxed them to Katherine and texted her to take a look.

She did some more research about fires in the city of Graysville and in the unincorporated areas, including the one where Rodney lived, and got several hits.

When she was exhausted, she tiptoed past Luke, who was asleep on the couch. She brushed her teeth and slipped into bed and then into slumber. Luke would probably wake up disappointed that they weren't sharing a bed, but it was better that way. This relationship, if that's what you called it, was moving a little too quickly.

At least now she wouldn't be lying to her mother when Barbara asked about her involvement with Luke. They really were together, or had been. But right now her primary focus had to be on finding the killer. Was it Rodney Willis? *I wonder where you are, right now, and just what you're doing.*

Chapter Thirteen

"Mary Louise Crabtree, what a beautiful name," Rodney said, adjusting the patch he'd taken to wearing to hide the bulk of his burn scars. "It's Southern, isn't it?" A safe bet, since she was enrolled in a Southern university. But more than a lucky guess.

"Yes, we're originally from Savannah, but my parents moved us down to Kissimmee, Florida, after I was in high school." Miss Mary Louise Crabtree was just a veritable fount of information.

He had cornered pretty little Mary Louise in the campus bookstore when he brushed up against her and caused her books to tumble to the floor. Of course, being the gentleman he was, he naturally helped her pick them up.

She'd winced at his disfigured face, but only for a second, and she had the good breeding and grace to hide her disgust. Too late. He'd seen it and she would pay for that dearly when he got her alone. She was no different from the rest of them. Looks were paramount to women like that. Beauty queens were the worst offenders. All those platitudes about beauty being skin deep was just hype. Beauty was everything.

He was handsome, or had been before the fire. His mother had always told him so. "My handsome little man" this, and "my handsome little man" that. She'd said it enough times he'd come to believe it. But now

172

that he had to live with his flaws, as he called them, pretty little things like Mary Louise Crabtree didn't want to have much, if anything, to do with him. He'd been on a few dates with some mousy girls, but they weren't his type. His type was the Mary Louise Crabtrees of this world. That was his birthright, his destiny. He just had to find the right one. The one who would appreciate him for who he really was.

"Thank you," Mary Louise said, as Rodney handed her the textbooks. She glanced around the store nervously, like she was expecting someone. But he could read her body language. The little bitch couldn't wait to get away from him.

"Go ahead, you can ask," Rodney prompted in a near whisper. "You're dying to know where I got these scars, aren't you?"

"No, I wasn't thinking that," she denied.

"It's okay. I'll tell you. I'm not ashamed. I got these scars serving my country, in a firefight over Iraq."

Mary Louise Crabtree turned to look at him. Not look past him. Not look away from him. But actually look right at him. She probably thought he was a flying ace. An officer. She never would have guessed he was just an enlisted grunt who'd served as a mechanic for the past year and received a dishonorable discharge for a little misunderstanding about a fire they accused him of starting but were never able to prove. He'd enlisted the day after the Melinda Crawford murder. It was a close call, but he had to get away. He'd shipped his brother off to an aunt in Jacksonville, and then he was home free.

"You poor thing. My brother is in Afghanistan. We're all terribly proud of him."

Gotcha, Rodney thought, looking back at the girl who had to be one of the stupidest, most pathetic of the homecoming contestants. She probably ranked just below his brother on the IQ scale. He was nothing if not prepared. He'd studied her, studied all of them, knew everything about them—where they were at night, what kind of naughty things they were doing and with whom, what their secrets were and their weaknesses, what lines would work on them and what lines wouldn't. Mary Louise would be a cakewalk. He wouldn't even need his brother to draw her out.

People warmed to Donny. They felt sorry for him. They genuinely liked him. They weren't afraid of him. But back to unspoiled little Mary Louise Crabtree.

"Yes, well, you know I don't regret what I did for my country, but I have to wear this patch because it covers up most of the scars. And these scars, they scare off most of the women I meet. Most of the women I meet wouldn't even be seen with me, let alone be caught dead drinking a cup of coffee with me, or having dinner with me. But I have a feeling you're different, Miss Mary Louise Crabtree. I have a feeling you're braver than most people. That you see beyond the surface, that you can gaze at a person and see straight into their hearts."

Mary Louise tipped her head in acknowledgement, offering that innocent, wide-mouthed smile that probably melted the hearts of the pageant judges.

"You would, wouldn't you?" Rodney prodded. "Have coffee with a veteran?"

May Louise hesitated for only the briefest moment before her benevolent compassion and good Southern breeding got the better of her.

"Of course."

"I'll walk you to the checkout, and then—my chariot awaits."

Maybe he *was* laying it on a bit thick. Probably he was a little above her capacity to appreciate his wit and charm, but this was his game and he'd play it the way he wanted to. It had worked so far. And Mary Louise was Lucky Number Seven, one of thirty tantalizing distractions until he could find a way to hit the jackpot.

Chapter Fourteen

When Luke got the call on his cell phone about the seventh victim, he was heading out of the law school parking lot. This last test had been brutal. He hadn't put in the time to study, but he had struggled through. Sometimes he wondered if going to law school was worth it. He enjoyed being a cop. He felt if he could just make detective, that might be the challenge he needed. But he had always seen the police department as a means to an end. Being a cop added a new dimension to, and a real life understanding of, the study of law. It would make him a better lawyer.

Of course, being a cop in Graysville was small potatoes. But as it turned out, Graysville was in the big leagues now that a serial killer was on the loose in his town. His law school buddies were more than curious about the case. It was a close-knit community. Many of them knew one or more of the dead girls personally. A couple of them were even dating girls who had competed in the homecoming pageant. The other students in the class were book smart, but they had no idea what went on in the underbelly of the city. He, on the other hand, was living the law every day he was out on the streets.

His mother wasn't too keen on him working as a cop. She thought his law school schedule was rigorous enough without his being burdened with a job. She'd also been pretty upset that his name had been dragged through the mud when Melinda Crawford was killed on his watch. She didn't understand that he would do whatever it took to make it right.

The memory of Flippy standing there over Melinda's body, in shock, kept coming back to him. What if it had been her lying there? What if the killer had murdered Flippy instead of Melinda? What if he hadn't gotten back just at that moment? Flippy might not be alive today, and Luke couldn't have lived with that.

He'd been a little brutal with her, dragging her down to the station for questioning right after Jack had been hurt, but he was more scared than angry. That's just how he showed it. It had been a close call, one he didn't want to repeat.

And if it was the same killer, what if he was still after Philippa? It made sense. He had discussed this at length with Chief Bradley and with Jack Hale and his wife. Actually, Jack Hale was not a bad guy. They had a lot in common. Both had backgrounds as cops; both were going to law school. And Crystal Ball Kate? What a knockout. No wonder Jack had been attracted to her and she was the world's darling. And brains—the woman had those in spades. She was fixated on the idea that Flippy was the target, and she talked about the killer's scars, although she didn't know if they were real scars or psychological scars. Her predictions weren't always specific, but since it was on her recommendation that Flippy was accorded police protection, he would always be grateful to her.

Chief Bradley had fallen under the spell of Crystal Ball Kate and would have given her the moon if she'd asked. So he had happily authorized the protective watch for Philippa. He had assigned Luke as her personal bodyguard, although Flippy didn't think she needed protection. But then neither had Melinda Crawford or Traci Farris or any of the other dead girls.

Katherine was spot-on about the latest victim, a beauty named Mary Louise Crabtree. They had surrounded the site of the body dump but had missed the killer by minutes. The media hadn't yet gotten hold of the news, but when they did, all hell would break loose, again. The vultures would be swarming around the girl's apartment, picking over scraps of maudlin interviews with those who had known her and those who hardly knew her. He dialed Flippy's number, then reconsidered. He wanted to tell her in person. Maybe he just wanted to see her again. She should be picking up her mother at the airport right about now, and he had arranged for his partner to tail her, although she didn't know it.

Chief Bradley had insisted he take the night off, since he was logging in so much overtime. He was beat and decided to take the chief up on his offer.

Perfect timing, since Flippy's mother was in town. Flippy would need to take action, hold a press conference, work her magic, kick some media butt. But not tonight.

He had to admit she was a pro at what she did. The reporters respected her, the families revered and depended on her. She was a natural. The university should be thankful they had her. But damned if he'd ever admit that to her.

He spent most of his time now scared to death someone was going to snatch her away. She probably thought he was gruff and uncaring, but he didn't want to make her nervous.

He couldn't wait until this whole ordeal was over, until the killer was dead or behind bars. And then he could breathe easy around Flippy.

Chapter Fifteen

Flippy watched the jet taxi down the runway at the Graysville Community Airport and then waited for her mother at baggage claim. It was a small airport, which made it easy to pick up passengers. Flippy typically traveled light, with only one carry-on bag in the overhead compartment and a purse. It didn't matter if Barbara was traveling for one night or ten nights, she'd need to check her luggage.

Barbara's face broke into a broad smile when she saw her daughter.

"Philippa," she cried.

"Mom," said Flippy, hugging her mother. "You don't mind if I call you Mom, do you?"

"Not here. I don't know anyone in this place." Missing in her description, but understood, was the word "godforsaken."

"It's so nice to see you. Do you have a hotel reservation for me?"

"Yes, at the Graysville Inn. It's not the Ritz, but it's nice. They serve fresh chocolate chip cookies at night. I had to pull in a favor to even get you a room. The networks have taken every available room in Graysville." Flippy took her mother's bag and carried it to the car. As soon as she'd mentioned the networks, she knew she'd made a mistake.

"The networks?" Barbara inquired. "Are they here

for that Homecoming Homicides case?"

Flippy frowned but didn't answer the question, and Barbara had already moved on to the next topic.

"So, when am I going to meet your young man?"

"Mom, you make him sound like something out of a Jane Austen novel. Actually, he does remind me of one of her characters. He's a real Boy Scout. Or more like Dudley Do-Right."

"Ooh, a Canadian Mountie. I can't wait to meet him. He sounds interesting. Is he good-looking?"

"Actually, I never thought about him in those terms, but yes, he's pretty spectacular."

"Not as cute as Jack, I'll wager."

"Well, let's face it, no one has a mug like Jack Armstrong."

"Or a body."

"Mom! You're naughty. Jack's available now, by the way, if you're interested. But Luke has other qualities. The best one is he's not a cheater. Or at least I don't think he is."

"Don't bring up your father on this trip."

"That was never my intention."

"I've been reading about that poor girl, your friend Traci."

"They had a memorial service for her yesterday. Actually it's been a pretty brutal couple of days."

"Well, I'm glad I'm here. I'm going to take you and Luke to a nice dinner. Did you make a reservation?"

"Yes. We really don't have any time to spare, but I got us in at a restaurant I think you'll like."

Flippy pulled out of the parking lot and caught up with her mother in the ten minutes it took to get to the hotel.

"You're looking good, Philippa," Barbara said.

"Luke thinks I'm too thin and that I don't eat enough. He likes his women to have some meat on their bones. That's how he puts it."

"Don't let yourself go. You still have some good years ahead of you. You might want to do some modeling."

"Mom, those days are over. I don't want to model. I don't want to enter any more beauty pageants, for heaven's sake. I have a job I like and I'm very good at it."

"Are we going to see your place first?"

"Well, I thought we could pick you up at your hotel later, then go over to Luke's, I mean our place, for some drinks and hors d'oeuvres and then out to dinner."

"That would be lovely. I'll have time for a quick beauty nap. Did you talk to your sister about the wedding yet?"

"Yes, I called her and told her she needed to stop acting out and let you have the wedding you want, even though it *is* her wedding."

"You didn't call her yet, did you?"

"Mom, I've been a little preoccupied. But I promise I'll do it tonight."

"Have you eaten lunch yet?" Flippy asked as they pulled up to the hotel.

"I had something before I got on the plane. I'm not hungry. I think I'll check into the hotel, freshen up, and wait for you to pick me up."

"We'll be by at around seven."

Flippy hugged her mother again and brought the luggage in to the front desk while her mother checked in. Then they said their goodbyes.

Flippy drove back to her office, only a few minutes away, and greeted the homeless guys in the front.

"You're back."

"The police picked us up," said a new man, a middle-aged guy who said his name was Chuck.

"Did they treat you okay?"

"They fed us, gave us some new clothes and blankets they had collected. But we couldn't stay there forever. We wanted to come back."

"That's good."

"I applied for a job," Chuck announced.

"That's wonderful. Doing what?"

"Well, working construction in one of those government works projects. It doesn't pay much. It will barely keep a roof over my head." Chuck laughed. "But it's respectable. I'm glad to have the work."

"What did you do before you got to Graysville?"

"I was an engineer, but I got laid off and I never could find another job."

"All you need is a break. Congratulations." Flippy made a mental note to ask Luke if he had any extra clothes he could spare for Chuck.

"Are you warm enough out here?"

"It'll be fine with our new blankets."

Flippy went to the office, got her messages from Misty, and waited for Luke to come by. They were going to stop at the outdoor chapel on Lake Mary. It was a famous university landmark and a favorite place for weddings. The chapel was beautiful and so was the view. Students picnicked there and tailgated during football season. An unlikely place for a body dump, but this killer was unpredictable. He had managed to elude them so far.

Luke came by and popped his head into her office.

"Ready?"

"Yes. I just dropped my mother off at the hotel."

"I've prepared the appetizers, and the wine is chilling."

"Thanks. I appreciate it."

"I had a cleaning service come by, so the place is spotless, except for Cruz. I hope she doesn't make a mess. Does your mother like dogs?"

"Not on her own carpet, but she's probably fine if they're peeing on someone else's carpet in someone else's house."

"Before I meet her, I need to ask you something. Are we supposed to be sleeping together?"

"What?"

"Well, I mean, I know we're sleeping together, well, we haven't technically slept in the same bed yet, but does she think we're sleeping together? I mean what is our relationship?"

"I don't know. What *is* our relationship?"

"Well, I know what I'd like it to be. You're my girlfriend. Are you okay with that?"

"That was pretty sudden, but yes, I'm okay with telling my mother that."

"But are *you* okay with that?"

"Yes." Flippy smiled, and he leaned over and kissed her.

"I saw that," Misty said. "Why is it all the good guys are taken?"

"I don't know. You seemed pretty chummy with the owner of DaVinci's."

"Oh, Riley? He's okay. But he's married to his job.

He's too serious."

"I'll bet he could be the right guy if you let him know you're interested."

"He knows, all right. But he isn't doing anything about it. You don't see any ring on this finger, do you?"

Luke smiled.

That reminded Flippy she needed to return the ring to Jack. She didn't want it anymore. Maybe she'd just put it in the mail. But no, that was too cold. She didn't hate Jack anymore. Maybe she could fix him up with Misty. No, she couldn't do that to Misty, not to any girl.

"I'll see you tomorrow, Misty."

"Bye, you two. Have fun."

Flippy waved to Chuck and the rest of the guys as she and Luke got into the car and drove off.

"Luke, did you get that list of current and former employees at the university, anyone who would have access to university buildings?"

Luke made the turn toward the chapel.

"Yes, it's in the file in the back seat. Why?"

"I just want to cross-check something."

"You have anything you want to share?"

"Just a hunch. Not yet. Thanks for bringing them back."

"The homeless guys?"

"You know who I mean."

"I had them checked out and deloused. Not really. Just clean and fed. Turns out a couple of them had pretty respectable jobs. It's just the economy. Everyone is down on their luck."

"You see, that's what I've been telling you."

"Maybe you're right. Maybe they are providing some protection for you. Safety in numbers."

They pulled into the park and drove up to the chapel.

"It's lovely here," Flippy said.

"Is this where you want our wedding?"

"You're crazy."

"Crazy about you."

Flippy blushed. "Are you going to charm my mother tonight?"

"I'm going to try to."

"She's pretty hard to please, but you're a pretty likeable guy."

"Thanks."

They walked to the chapel. There was a lot of activity. Students studying, walking hand in hand, reading.

"This location might be just a little too busy for him," Flippy noted.

"But he's clever. He could drive up, blend in for a while and when no one's around, make his move."

"We can't rule it out," Flippy said. "It would be horrific to put a dead body in this beautiful place."

"That's what would appeal to his inner sickness," Luke said, making more notes. "I think we have every possible landmark location staked out. But we have to find him before he dumps the bodies. He doesn't kill them here. He does it somewhere else. I've got my guys tailing every one of the girls who is still living in Graysville. It's going to be hard for him to snatch anyone. I guess we'd better head home so we can get dressed and pick up your mother."

When they got to Luke's condo, Flippy grabbed the list from Luke's car. She was anxious to see if Rodney Willis was on it, but Luke snatched the file first.

"Tonight is about us—and your mother. We've had enough work for today." The file lay on the living room table. Cruz was nipping at their heels.

"Let me take her out," Luke said, "while you start getting ready."

Flippy went into the guest room to change. When she came out, she found Luke and Cruz in his bedroom.

Luke emerged from his bathroom in a tailored suit that made him look like a model out of *Gentlemen's Quarterly*.

"Wow," she said. "You look great. I didn't know you owned a suit."

"I own several," Luke said. "And you, well, you look amazing, like a beauty queen."

Flippy laughed. She had taken a long time dressing to impress Luke and her mother. She was still trying to impress her mother.

Cruz was nipping at Luke's heels.

"Cruz, sorry, girl, you'll have to wait here. We'll be right back. I'll bring you a nice juicy bone," he promised.

"Flip, I noticed your engagement ring is still in the box in your room."

"I'm planning to give it back or send it back. I just haven't gotten around to it."

Luke smiled.

They arrived at the hotel right on time, and Barbara was waiting in the lobby.

"Mom, this is Luke Slaughter. Luke this is my mother, Barbara Tannenbaum."

"What a knockout," Luke raved. "Like mother like daughter."

Barbara blushed. "Well, aren't you sweet to say

that. Did Philippa tell you I was a beauty queen, too?"

"I can see where Philippa gets her good looks," Luke said.

Luke wound his arm around Flippy's elbow and then around Barbara's and led them out to the car. "Your carriage awaits."

"I like him," whispered Barbara. Barbara was impressed with Luke's car, too. By the time they arrived at the condo, Luke had Barbara eating out of his hand.

She was more than impressed with the condo.

"Flippy, this is wonderful. I'm so happy you live in such a nice place. This must have cost a fortune. I know you're not taking any money from your father. How can you afford this?"

"I make a good salary, Mom. And, well, Luke won't take any money from me."

Barbara smiled her approval. "Well, I'll have a good report to take to your father. He's convinced you live in a dump and that you're practically out on the streets because you're broke."

Flippy almost choked. "Well, you can see that's not the case. Tell your husband I'm doing just fine without his money."

"You shouldn't talk about your father like that," Barbara admonished. Luke gave Barbara a tour of the condo and she commented on all the furnishings.

"I couldn't have decorated this better myself."

"Flippy did most of it," Luke said, and she made a face at him behind her mother.

"Why didn't I know about these hidden talents?"

"Your daughter is more than just beautiful," Luke answered. "She has great taste." Then he whispered in

Flippy's ear, licking it, "And she tastes good." Flippy kicked him.

When he showed Barbara his room and the guest room, Flippy could see the wheels spinning in her mother's head: Who sleeps where? Do they sleep separately, or are the two rooms just for show?

Then Cruz trotted out, and Barbara took to the dog right away.

"Mrs. Simmons has a Bichon, and she says they don't shed."

Cruz kept getting underfoot, but Luke dazzled her mother with his appetizers and the wine he served.

"He's a keeper," Barbara said when Luke left the room.

They had a lovely time at dinner. Luke did the ordering, and the food was superb, right down to the desserts. And Flippy did have a dessert—a very chocolately, fattening one with whipped cream on top. The service was excellent, and Luke picked up the very hefty tab.

"Luke, you don't need to do that. My mother was going to take us out."

"I can afford it. And Barbara is our guest."

What could have been a disastrous evening turned out to be one of the most pleasant times she had ever spent with her mother. Barbara was careful not to mention Jack once, and by the end of the evening she had accepted Luke into the family.

"So what are your intentions toward my daughter?" Barbara asked.

"Mom, don't put Luke on the spot."

"I'd love to answer that question, honey."

"Honey?" Flippy looked at Luke.

"Yes, darling, why don't we make our little announcement now."

"What?"

"I know we said we'd wait, but Mrs. Tannenbaum, Flippy and I are getting married and we wanted you to be the first to know."

"Luke!" Flippy pushed her chair back and stood up.

"I know it's kind of sudden, but I love your daughter and she loves me, and it just feels right."

"Aren't you laying it on a bit thick?" Flippy whispered, pinching his arm.

"I'm serious."

Barbara nearly fell out of her chair. She practically screamed. "Wait until I tell your father. Philippa, Luke, I'm so happy. Have you set a date yet?"

"Mom, this is news to me. Luke just sprang this little surprise on me."

"She's just joking, Barbara. We haven't set a date yet, but we'd like it to be as soon as possible."

When Barbara went to the powder room, Flippy grabbed Luke's arm.

"What the hell are you doing? I said we were dating, I didn't need you to fake a marriage proposal."

"I'm not faking it. I want to marry you, and now that I've told your mother, it's a done deal. She'd be so disappointed if you turned me down."

"Luke, you're insane. I'm not going to discuss this. You're in big trouble. As soon as we drop my mother off, you're going to find out just how much."

Luke grinned. "It was worth it just to see the horrified look on your face when I told her."

"So this is all just a big joke to you."

"I said I was serious. I love you. I am asking you to marry me, for real."

Flippy shook her head. "I don't know what to make of you. I just broke off my engagement to one man. I'm not ready to jump back into bed with another man."

"You could have fooled me." Luke laughed.

Barbara sailed back into the room, looking as happy as a bride.

"I can't wait to start making plans. What are we going to do tomorrow?"

"Mom, I'm going to have to work, and so is Luke. Why don't we have breakfast and spend some time together for a while in the morning, and then you can come to my office."

Barbara was chattering away in the car, while Flippy was stoic, refusing to talk directly to Luke.

As Luke dropped Barbara off at her hotel, she called out, "I'll see you two lovebirds in the morning." Which was code for "I don't care if you two are sharing a room, now that you're engaged."

When Flippy and Luke were alone, she turned to him.

"You've flipped out, Luke Slaughter. There's no engagement and there's going to be no wedding."

"You try telling that to Barbara."

"This is outrageous."

"Do you love me?"

"How can I love you? We've only been together two times."

"Technically, it's more than that."

Flippy elbowed him in the car.

"You'll learn to love me," he said.

"You're impossible. Let's go home."

When they got home, Cruz met them at the door.

"I'll walk Cruz and then we'll talk," Luke said.

Flippy had other ideas. She grabbed the file Luke had brought home and went into her bedroom to change into her pajamas. And she locked the door. She settled onto the bed and started perusing the list. It was pages long, covering employees, ex-employees... There were thousands of names on the list. She turned the pages until she got to the Ws and held her breath.

Sure enough, there he was, the bastard. Rodney Willis. He was a janitor for the university. And in that position, he had easy access to all the buildings, including the stadium. Gotcha. She circled his name. She needed to dig deeper, but he was the best lead they had. She was going to make sure it was him before she told Luke, who was knocking at her door.

"Flippy, open up."

"I'm going to sleep now. Go away."

"Please," Luke said. "Open up for me."

"I have nothing to say to you."

"Let me get this straight. You're mad at me because I said I love you and want to marry you? That doesn't make any sense."

"You're the one who is not making sense."

"Where's the file I brought home?"

"It's in here, but I've gone through it and there are no matches. See you in the morning."

Flippy heard a noise at the keyhole. Luke was opening the door with a key.

"Get out of my room."

"Technically it's *my* room."

"And you're breaking and entering, invading my privacy."

"One of my many law enforcement skills," he said as he pushed open the door.

"Get away from me."

"No." Luke edged into the room, hearing capitulation in her voice. "You want me. You know you do. So don't deny it."

"You are so sure of yourself. I don't even know you. I'm not marrying you."

Luke covered the space between the door and her bed in seconds, sat down, and gathered her into his arms.

"Philippa. We can talk about this later. But don't go to bed mad." He kissed her then, a long, searching kiss, and she softened. He was a great kisser.

He started undressing her, and met with little resistance.

"This doesn't mean anything," she whispered without conviction.

"It means something to me."

Flippy sighed and let him finish what he started.

"I'm sleeping in here tonight," Luke stated.

"Suit yourself."

Luke laughed.

"You'll come around. You'll see."

Luke kissed her and turned off the light. He forgot all about the file. He'd tell her about the latest body in the morning. Tonight she needed her beauty sleep.

Chapter Sixteen

"Wake up Sleeping Beauty," Rodney crooned, coaxing the naked, drugged girl awake, stroking her face delicately, smoothing the skin on her left cheek.

"So soft and round, such beautiful skin," Rodney whispered. "You got your beauty rest, and now we need some quality time together. We have so much to talk about."

The girl moaned and woke with a start when she saw Rodney standing over her—a monster with a knife in his hands. She struggled to get out of her bonds, but they were too tight. She was tied to a hard board and staring into harsh lights.

"It's okay, baby. Oh, does this knife bother you? No need for that. Let me put that away...for now. He placed the knife gingerly on the table next to a tray of tools.

He picked up a package of matches and lit one, letting it flicker dangerously close to the girl's left cheek.

She tried to wriggle away.

Rodney petted her breasts with one hand.

"Calm down, now, kitten. Kitten. Isn't that what your friends call you? Their pet name for Kitty. Kitty Bailey. What a beauty. Now stop struggling for me, Kitty Cat, and I won't burn you. Wouldn't want to ruin that beautiful face, now would we?"

"Why are you doing this?" Kitty cried, shrinking back from the monster's face.

"Oh, that's right. You haven't seen my face before. It was my big brother you met. Well, Donny's not here anymore. It's just me. You and me. And you'd better get used to this face, doll, 'cause it's the last one you're going to see."

Kitty struggled against the ropes.

"Uh, uh, I've got a feisty one here." Rodney loosened the ropes. "All right, sugar, calm down, now. You and me, we're going to get on just fine, if you cooperate. If you don't, well, I think you know what's going to happen to you.

"Now, I'm going to untie you, Kitty Cat, but don't get any ideas. There's no one going to hear you scream. This place is locked down tight. We're out in the middle of nowhere, the End of the World. But if you do what I say, exactly what I say, you're going to be all right. Now, scoot on over to the dressing room. You'll find a fresh pair of panties and a bra. I think Queenie was about your size, and we'll start with the wedding gown."

Kitty was shaking, but she walked into the dressing room and, minutes later, came out dressed in a white silk gown.

Rodney turned on the microphone. "Donny, you can come on in now. The competition is about to start. I'll put on the music."

"And you," he said, grabbing Kitty's arm roughly. "If you scream, if you so much as say one word, you'll be sorry. Do we understand each other, Kitty Cat?" he said, purring and stroking her left cheek.

Kitty blanched and bobbed her head.

"Now go on, walk on up the runway, and let's get this show started."

"You ready, Donny? You got your camera? Now, I want some great shots today for my collection. Doesn't she look great, big brother? Doesn't she look like Queenie?"

"She does, Rodney. She's wearing Mama's wedding dress. It's the showstopper."

"You are so right, Donny."

"Now, show us what you've got, sweetheart."

Kitty walked up the runway and onto the stage.

"Don't be so stiff. Show some life, now, darlin'," Rodney said. "You make a beautiful bride."

Chapter Seventeen

When Flippy and Luke swung by the Graysville Inn to pick up Barbara, her mother was full of wedding plans. Luke spent most of the morning laughing, while Flippy was mostly close-mouthed and sulking. She had only one thing on her mind, and that was to find Rodney Willis. He was out there, plotting his dastardly deeds, zeroing in on his next victim, maybe he already had her. But this time, she was one step ahead of him. She wasn't even going to consult Luke, she was so sure about this.

She'd gotten a text from Katherine to be careful. And she would be.

Besides, Luke had gone off the deep end. He was discussing china patterns and invitations with Barbara. She didn't want any part of it. She couldn't make her move until she got her mother on that plane today, but then she was going to break this case wide open and break it off with Luke. She was getting far too comfortable with him, way too quickly. After all, it was just a game to Luke, a ruse to throw her mother off track.

She had already made a call earlier to get her director's permission to obtain access to Rodney's file in the university personnel office.

"I think I've got him," Flippy told the director, and proceeded to outline her reasons.

"Philippa. Great work. Have you shared your findings with Luke or Chief Bradley?"

"Not yet."

"Don't," the director advised. "I know what I said about being a team player, but I want us to crack this case."

"My feelings exactly," Flippy agreed.

"But I don't want you to take any risks. This man is dangerous. Review his file, make sure we have a solid case, and then you and I will go to Chief Bradley and take him down."

Flippy was going to do better than that. She was going to find out all she needed to know. And she'd have the case all sewn up and presented to Luke on a silver platter, not as a wedding present, but maybe as a peace offering for putting up with her mother, letting her stay in his condo, and for being such an all-around Boy Scout and nice guy. In spite of his touchy-feely tendencies, she hadn't lost sight of that. He was the real thing. She could make a life with him. But on her terms. He was sweeping her off her feet and she was losing control. Out of the frying pan and into the fire. She wasn't ready for a new relationship. She had only to look at her parents' mess of a marriage to see that.

This morning she had taken Jack's ring out of the box and slipped it back on her finger, just to see how it felt. It felt like a betrayal to Luke, so she slipped it into her skirt pocket. She was going to return it to Jack before the day was out.

"Personally, I prefer a June wedding," Luke was saying.

"I totally agree, if we can rebook The Atlanta Botanical Garden."

"Mom," Flippy protested. She wasn't seriously proposing to use the same place where she had been scheduled to marry Jack. But Luke didn't know that. He'd hate it if he knew.

"I'm only saying that Philippa loves flowers. And it's a beautiful venue."

"I'd marry Flippy anywhere, even at a campground."

That brought the conversation to a halt in a hurry.

Barbara glared at Flippy.

"No, I didn't tell him, Mom. Honest. That's just a random remark."

"What?" Luke gave Flippy a puzzled look.

"Don't ask," Barbara and Flippy said in unison.

"Well, then The Atlanta Botanical Garden sounds wonderful," Luke said.

Flippy sighed. Why didn't her mother just arrange the rest of her life? She'd done that since Flippy was a little girl. Natalie was silly to fight the force that was Barbara. Barbara was like the tide. She kept rolling in, rolling over everything in her path, and there was no use resisting.

"By the way, did you call your sister yet?" Barbara asked.

"No, but I promise I will."

"Well, hold off on that call, except to congratulate Natalie."

"Why?"

"Last night I got to thinking that Natalie should have the kind of wedding she wants. I'll be occupied with your wedding, so if she wants to get married around a campfire, so be it. Who am I to stand in the way of true love?"

"Who are you, and what have you done with my mother?"

Barbara smiled.

"You know, Flippy, I called your father, and he would like me to come home early, so I booked a morning flight. We have just enough time to make it. I won't be able to see your office."

Did the relief on Flippy's face show? She had dreaded the next few hours. Barbara meeting Misty, seeing where her daughter worked, and discovering her involvement with the Homecoming Homicides case. The less her mother knew about her job, the better. And she was focused on only one thing—finding Rodney Willis.

"Why does Dad want you home early?"

There were tears in Barbara's eyes.

"I think I should make my exit," said Luke. "I'll be waiting in the car if you need me." Luke hugged Barbara. "Barbara, it was wonderful to meet you. I'm looking forward to spending some time with you and your husband in Atlanta, scouting out venues."

Seriously? When had that happened? Her mother and her pseudo fiancé were bonding, and that spelled disaster for Flippy. Luke was laying it on a bit thick.

Flippy turned her attention to her mother.

"Mom, why are you crying?"

"Well, last night when I told your father about your wedding, things got sentimental. You know, our little girls getting married at the same time, and then we got to talking about *our* wedding and our life, and one thing led to another and we spoke honestly for the first time in a long time."

"What do you mean?"

"I know you've been at odds with your father because you thought he was cheating on me. And I let you believe that because I wanted you on my side. But what you didn't know is the reason he's been cheating on me. I cheated on him first."

"Mom? No!"

Flippy was flabbergasted. It was the last admission she expected from her mother. As demanding and outrageous as Barbara was, she was not a cheater.

Barbara buried her face in her napkin to soak up her tears.

"I was ashamed to admit that to you. And there's more. I cheated on him around the time your brother was born. Neil is not your father's biological son."

Flippy's world split open.

"Does Dad know?"

"Of course he does. But he loves your brother as if he were our own. It was a time in our marriage that I was feeling fragile. I thought your father didn't love me. He was so consumed with work, and I felt I was losing my looks. I know it's shallow, but I took up with another man. It's not important who. But I got pregnant, and your father stayed with me."

Flippy narrowed her eyes.

"Am I?"

"Oh, yes, you are your father's. That part about the make-up sex, that's all true. Your father was plenty mad. His pride was hurt, and he had his flings along the way. Who's to say it wouldn't have happened anyway? But I poisoned your mind against your father, and for that, I'm truly sorry."

"I don't know what to say. Does Neil know?"

"No and I hope to God he never finds out. Neil and

your father are joined at the hip. What good would telling Neil about my indiscretion do? He'd hate me forever. Believe me, Philippa, I'm ashamed of what I did, and that's why I've tolerated your father's dalliances. Because that's all they were. Your father loves me. I don't deserve his love, but he loves me. I think he just did it to get back at me. But that's all changed now. We're letting our daughters set the example. He's promised never to stray again. And I believe him."

"Wow. This is a lot to process."

"Do you hate me?"

Flippy was at a loss for words. Hate was a strong word.

"All these years, I've been blaming Dad," she began. "That was unfair to me and to him. Turns out he wasn't such a monster after all. But that doesn't let him off the hook. Mom, I hate to spoil your homecoming, but the real reason I cut Dad out of my life was because one afternoon I came home from school break and I found Dad and Lissie Hathaway in your bed. Lissie Hathaway is my age, for heaven's sake. He was sleeping with a girl young enough to be his daughter. Did you know that?"

Barbara didn't look surprised.

"I suspected it, and then I confronted him. He came clean because he was so sorry for having upset you."

"Then why didn't you talk to me about it? I was horrified and I couldn't tell you."

"Your father was ashamed of his behavior, and he promised never to betray our marriage again. And honestly, I don't think he has since. And besides, you earned your own way. He was proud of you. But he knew if he told you the truth you'd turn against me, and he wouldn't do that to me."

Flippy and her mother had a good cry and then hugged.

"Mom, I shouldn't forgive you, but I love you. Tell Dad we'll talk when I come to Atlanta."

"You'll bring Luke, of course."

"As long as we're being honest… About Luke…"

"Flippy, that man adores you. It's written all over his face. And I love him for that. True love is something that's too precious to discard."

"Well, you loved Jack, too, Mom. What if Luke turns out to be just like Jack?"

"He won't. I can tell. He's solid, Flippy. Don't let him get away, if you love him, too."

Did she love Luke? She didn't want to admit it to herself, but she *was* falling in love with him. She knew she wouldn't have slept with him if she didn't have deep feelings for him. Being inebriated was just an excuse. She knew exactly what she was doing at all times. Well, most times.

Flippy dried her eyes, and they walked out to meet Luke.

After they dropped Barbara off at the airport, Flippy sat back in the car and relaxed.

"Thanks."

"For what?"

"For being so great with Barbara, um, my mother."

"I genuinely like her. You should give her a chance too."

"You know, you are really a good guy."

"I've been trying to tell you that."

"I think I could even love you."

Luke turned to Flippy and pressed her hand against his cheek. "You love me?"

Flippy placed her hand over his. "You're hard *not* to love. But we have to take it slower. I have to be sure. I can't go through another disappointment."

"Well, you know, the last time you were disappointed, it worked out pretty well for me, so I don't regret what happened."

"It's random the way things work out, isn't it?"

Luke swung by the doughnut shop and bought a dozen doughnuts. When they arrived at Flippy's office, he distributed most of them to the homeless men and put the rest of the box on Misty's desk. Misty held out a fistful of pink slips.

"All these messages for me?" Flippy asked.

"The phone hasn't stopped ringing since I got in this morning."

Flippy turned to Luke.

"You know, I really don't need you to babysit me. I'm fine here. I know you have work and school and a million things you need to be doing. And so do I. So you can leave."

"I do have to check things back at the station. You promise you won't leave here without telling me? I'll be back in a couple of hours." He couldn't tell her about the latest dead body, not yet.

"Scout's honor," Flippy said, doing the two-finger salute.

"Misty, you make sure your boss doesn't leave this office—and if she does, you call me," Luke said, pressing his card into Misty's hand. "Here's my number." Then he planted a big, noisy, wet kiss on Flippy's lips.

"Will do, Tiger," Misty replied.

"What is it about you and tigers?" Flippy wondered.

Luke sauntered out the door.

"Wow!" said Misty. "That's all I can say. You are so lucky. I hope you know that."

"I'm beginning to realize that," Flippy said.

Flippy went into her office. After a call to the university attorney and several reminder calls to the personnel office, she went to the fax machine and scanned it as the pages started rolling out.

Rodney Willis' personnel file. It was all there. He looked good for the crimes. He had applied to NFU and been rejected, but years later they had hired him as a building maintenance man. So he had access to all the sites, could move about the campus without causing alarm. There was a picture of the slime ball. But it wasn't the man who asked for her autograph at the pageant. She was so sure he had been the one. He sort of looked like the guy she had seen, but no, he wasn't. The guy she'd seen didn't have much hair under that baseball cap, and he was heavy set. Rodney Willis had a headful of dark hair and was good looking, at least from his profile. At least he had been a good-looking man at one time. But the left side of his face was scarred. And he had started the fire that burned his house down. He was a fire starter. He worked at the university. His mother was a beauty queen. He still lived at the same address. They must have rebuilt on the same land. There was a connection here, but not all the pieces fit. Maybe Luke could help her sort it out, but Luke would go all cowboy on her and try to bust the door down and ride to the rescue and probably get himself killed.

She could ask him to arrange to have the house watched or tail Rodney Willis. But what if she was wrong? What if Rodney Willis was just a law-abiding citizen and the police came in full force and arrested or shot the wrong man? She had to proceed cautiously. She knew she should call the director with the confirmation. But she had to be absolutely sure.

She needed to check things out, from a safe distance, of course. But how was she going to get away from Misty, Luke's appointed watchdog?

She couldn't take her car keys, because if Misty noticed her car missing, she'd alert Luke. She wouldn't take her purse at all, just a few dollars and some change. The city bus ran right by her office, and she'd check the route. If it went out to the Willis place, she could ride the bus out there, scope out the situation, and call Luke. She wouldn't do anything hasty or stupid. Flippy called City Transportation and asked some questions about the Number 5 Bus Route. Yes, it went directly to the Willis place. That was the last stop on the route. The universe was cooperating.

Flippy took the file with the university names out of her briefcase and left it on her desk. She unwrinkled the newspaper article from her purse and wrote down the Willis address on a pad of paper. Then she tore off the top sheet and stuck the article and faxed copy of Rodney Willis' personnel history into the file so she'd have all the proof she needed when she went to Luke. Now that she had everything prepared, she walked into the outer office.

"Uh, Misty, I'm sort of hungry. I'm going to take a break and get a fresh slice from DaVinci's. I'll be right back."

"Tell Riley I said hi."

"You need to tell him the way you feel, Misty. Honesty is always the best policy. You'd be surprised what can happen."

Misty looked like she was considering it.

"Hold down the fort."

Flippy came out of her office and chatted a few minutes with Chuck and the rest of the guys.

"How's the new job going?"

"Oh, I don't start till tomorrow," Chuck reported.

There was a new man in the bushes today. She guessed they were a transient bunch. A new man moved in, another left. She waved to the new guy. He waved back.

"Thanks for the doughnuts," the man said.

"Actually, you can thank my friend Luke."

"Well, thank your friend Luke, then. They were much appreciated."

Flippy wanted to stay and talk, but she had a lot to accomplish.

She walked down the street toward DaVinci's, but instead of walking into the pizza joint, she turned the corner and sat at the bus stop and waited.

Chapter Eighteen

He was always one step ahead. That's how he kept the law at bay. That's what kept him on his toes in this race. This was a marathon, not a sprint, and he had not yet crossed the finish line.

By now, they would have found the body. It was so predictable, it was beginning to be routine. Pick up Number Seven, drop her off, begin the hunt for the next contestant—the lovely Kitty Bailey. She had looked beautiful in Queenie's wedding dress. And that's how he'd left her, propped up in the moonlight at the chapel. Two girls in as many days. He was moving up the schedule. That would confound them. The Kitty Cat capture had not gone exactly according to plan. She had tried to escape and had tripped on Queenie's high heels and fallen face down off the stage. The little hellcat had broken her neck before he'd completed his plans. Before he'd burned her face. Before she'd completed her modeling shots. Before the bathing suit competition. Donny had cried and tried to revive her.

He'd had to calm the sniveling idiot down before he dealt with Kitty. Well, she was already in the wedding gown, so what better place than the chapel.

He didn't even bother to wrap her body. He instructed Donny to pick her up, and they drove down to the chapel. Donny helped him place the bride. It was lovely, really.

"Now, not a word to anyone about this, big brother."

Donny sniffled. "It's our secret. Just like you told me."

"That's right. Now let's go back and develop the film. I think we got some great shots for my workroom. But first, I have a stop to make."

Rodney was restless. The Kitty Bailey incident had been totally unsatisfying. His lust for blood had been denied. He and Donny drove around the campus. Not many women out and about. Not when there was a serial killer on the loose. Chancing a visit to any of the sorority houses was out of the question, but some of the contestants had refused protection and insisted on staying off-campus.

He checked the homecoming program. Who was next? Dana something or other. There were almost too many to keep track of. Let them think he was the greatest serial killer of all time. The serial-killing prize goes to Rodney Willis with a total of thirty kills—no, make that thirty-one, if you include Melinda Crawford, thirty-two if you count Philippa Tannenbaum. Obfuscate. Throw them off the trail of his real target, the only girl who mattered.

Rodney flipped on the left-turn signal. "Here it is, Donny. I believe this is the address. Yes, the light's on, so she must be home. Now, remember how we practiced. You walk up to her door and tell her your car broke down and ask if you can use her phone to call your brother."

He watched Donny lumber out of the passenger seat, walk up to the house, and knock on the door. In a moment the lovely Dana appeared, and she handed over her phone to Donny. Donny turned around and looked back at the car.

"The handkerchief," Rodney called out.

Donny turned back to Dana, who was showing signs she was getting suspicious.

"I thought you said you had to call your brother."

This was almost too easy.

Rodney flew up the steps and took the handkerchief from his brother's pocket.

"Miss, I'm so sorry about this. My brother is, well, he's a little slow. Our car did break down, but I'm fixing it. All I need is a jack. You don't happen to have one of those, do you?"

Dana looked up and down the dark, deserted street.

"Well, no matter," Rodney said smoothly. I'll try another house. Sorry to have troubled you, miss."

Dana breathed a sigh of relief and smiled. Then she turned her back on Rodney to go back inside. That moment of hesitation was all Rodney needed. He grabbed her from behind and held the handkerchief up to her face. She sagged against him.

"Rodney, your girlfriend fell asleep," Donny asked. "Is she okay?"

"Sure, Donny. She just passed out. We need to get her home and take care of her, so help me get her into the back seat."

Donny picked her up as easily as if she were a ragdoll and placed her gingerly in the back seat of the car.

"You can sleep now," Donny said.

"Good job, bro. Now, shut her door, and let's get back home and prepare for our next contestant. She's a real beauty, isn't she?"

Donny smiled. "She is real pretty."

Rodney drove along. He needed a new challenge. Not that it wasn't fun carving them up and tossing them in campus drop zones, but it was so predictable, and the cops couldn't figure it out. He could have called and invited them to the party himself and they'd still be stymied. They deserved the hassle, just for being such bunglers.

For years he'd been looked over, scorned, cast off, rebuffed by girls just like Dana. And payback was sweet. So, maybe these particular girls hadn't offended him, but they were all the same type. A type that needed to be taught a lesson. *Beauty's only skin deep, yeah, yeah, yeah.*

Take Traci Farris, for example. A first-class slut if there ever was one. And Traci's recklessness had gotten the bus driver killed, too. Rodney had nothing against the city worker. The man was just collateral damage.

Anyone who would snake her best friend's man got what was coming to her. If *he'd* been in Philippa's shoes, he'd have killed her right there in bed, along with her worthless fiancé.

When Philippa found out what he had done for her, she would thank him. And he'd give her a chance to thank him for killing off the competition in the person of one super-bitch Melinda Crawford, who so didn't deserve the title of Homecoming Queen. But thanks to him, justice was served.

And then, sweet, pure, heartbroken Philippa Tannenbaum made her first mistake. Getting drunk and picking up a guy in a bar—not just any guy, either. The cop who'd been "protecting" Melinda Crawford. He'd been so disappointed in her, he wanted to wring her little neck. All women were tarts. She'd have to be taught a lesson, but he wouldn't make her suffer too much. She could be saved. He would grant her a last-minute reprieve, and she'd be so grateful to him she would be willing to do anything. He was sure of it.

After all, he was saving himself for her. He hadn't been with any of the women. He'd been tempted with the others, but he'd held back because she was worth the wait. That Boy Scout Luke Skywalker was another matter. He'd have to be dealt with severely. No mercy. First Philippa would wander into his trap, and then the hero would come riding to her rescue, and *boom*, end of story. He hadn't decided exactly how it would play out yet. But he had a schedule to keep. Couldn't keep Contestant Number Nine waiting. Or was it Number Ten?

Chapter Nineteen

"Luke, it's Misty. I think you'd better get over here."

"Misty, thank God. I've been trying to call Philippa forever, and all I get is her voice mail message. She must have turned her cell phone off. Or she's not answering for some reason. Where have you been? I've been trying to reach you, too. Is everything all right?"

"I'm not sure. I uh, went out for a few minutes—next door to talk to Riley at DaVinci's. Because Flippy said I had to be honest about my feelings, so I confronted Riley and told him how I feel, and he told me he felt the same about me and, guess what, we're together now."

"I'm happy for you, really happy, but where's Flippy? I have an important message for her. Write it down and give this information to Flippy and to Director Beckham. We got a call from a bus driver in training who's been riding the routes, shadowing the regular drivers. When he saw Traci Farris' picture in the news, he recognized her as a girl he'd seen at the bus stop that Monday night. A week later she turns up dead, and the regular bus driver was missing, so he figures he should call us. He's down at the station now, giving his statement. Crystal Ball Kate says she's seen a house in a vision that fits the description of the one at the end of that route. She said Flippy faxed some information over to her about a man named Rodney Willis. Did she say anything to you about it?

"No, I never heard that name."

"Will you put Flippy on the line?"

"Well, I would, if she were here, but I can't find her."

"What do you mean you can't find her? She's missing?"

"Well she went out for a slice of pizza, but Riley said she never came in to DaVinci's."

"Jesus, Misty. It was your job to keep an eye on her. I told you to call me if—"

"I am calling you, NOW."

"All right. Okay. Now where do you think she could have gone?"

"I have no idea. Her purse is still here. Her keys are still here. And she left her cell phone. Her car is still parked in the lot."

"Don't leave the phone. She might call you. I'm on my way."

Chapter Twenty

Was that the new homeless man at the back of the bus? No, Flippy's eyes were playing tricks on her. She'd only seen him once. When she stared at him, he looked the other way. It had to be someone else. Steadily, people got on and off the bus. It was a busy route, but as the bus veered out of town, there were only three people left on the bus, besides the driver. The homeless man, or the man who looked like the homeless man. And another man, a boy, really. He looked like a boy. Why, he was the boy who had asked for her autograph at the pageant. She had worked with the police forensic artist, and he'd done a composite sketch. It was the same face. His hair wisped out from under a baseball cap, and he had on the same outfit he wore the night of the pageant. He even had the same camera around his neck. As she studied him, he flashed a killer smile, a smile that would knock your socks off. And he was coming over to sit next to her.

This wasn't Rodney Willis. But it was the man at the pageant who had asked for her autograph. This boy was no killer. She was sure of it.

"I'm Donny. I live at 5555 Skyline Road." He pointed to a crumpled piece of paper pinned to his shirt, then pressed his hand to his heart. His coat was blocking the note so she couldn't read it.

"Hello, Donny."

"You're pretty. My mama was real pretty."

"Thank you." What was happening here? Who was this person?

"I saw your picture."

"You saw my picture, where?"

"Don't you remember me? You signed your picture."

"At the pageant? Do you mean I autographed my picture for you in the pageant program?"

"You signed your picture." Donny smiled again.

"What did you say your name was?"

"Donny. Donny Willis."

Flippy's heart raced.

"Do you have a brother?"

"My brother was supposed to pick me up, but he's at work. He cleans the buildings."

My God! This is the mentally-challenged brother of Rodney Willis. That's the connection. She needed to tell Luke right away, but in her haste, she'd left her cell phone in the office. *Stupid.*

"You said your mother was real pretty. Tell me about her."

"She was a beauty queen," Donny said. "I loved my mother. She took real good care of me. But then she got burned up. So now my brother takes care of me. Would you like to see my house?"

"Well, uh, I don't know."

"I want you to see my house. It's at the End of the World."

"The end of the world?"

"That's where I live. The End of the World."

If she could get into the house, she could tell for sure if a serial killer lived there. She wished she had told the director she had gone to check out the Willis house. But if anything happened, the director had Rodney's name and she'd know where to look.

"Is your brother home?"

"My brother cleans buildings at the university. He's at work now."

She raised her voice to get the bus driver's attention.

"How often does this bus run?"

"We run this route every thirty minutes."

A plan was beginning to form in Flippy's head. She could get off with Donny for just a few minutes, look around the house before the brother got home, then ride the bus back to the office and call Luke and the director.

"We got lots of nice things in the house. Things you would like to see."

"Well, Donny, I think I might like that. I can only stay for a few minutes, though."

Donny's smile shone.

She and Donny got off the bus, but the house wasn't close to the bus stop. It was a long walk. Trees covered the walkway like a canopy, dark and dense. By the time they got to the series of wooden structures at the end of the road, Flippy was winded. This was beginning to turn out to be a bad idea. By the time she saw the house and walked back to the stop, the thirty minutes would be gone. She'd have to catch the next bus. But it would be worth it if she could gather some evidence.

"This is the last stop—The End of the World," Donny said.

Flippy hoped it wasn't *her* last stop.

The house was a ramshackle series of wooden buildings, some single story, some two stories. None of them matched architecturally. The back portion looked older and was a burned-out jumble. The front part of the house was more modern. One of the structures was circular and seemed out of place. Donny walked through the door in front of her.

"Would you like a pop?"

"A pop?"

Donny led her to the refrigerator and held up a bottle of orange soda. "A pop."

"Oh, a soda pop. Okay."

Donny smiled. It was definitely not the smile of a serial killer. He handed her the bottle.

"Do you have an opener?"

He produced a bottle opener, and she opened the bottle and placed the opener back on the table. She took a drink. The long walk through the woods had made her thirsty.

"Can I see the rest of the house?"

"I'll take you on a tour. Usually Rodney does the tour. But he's at work. He cleans buildings for the university. He was supposed to pick me up, but he was late."

Donny led the way through a threadbare living room, undecorated except for a lace doily and, on the doily, a picture of a beautiful woman.

"Is this your mother?"

"My mother was real pretty, just like you. That's my mother."

Flippy picked up the picture to get a better look. Gracie Willis was beyond pretty. She was beautiful. Or had been.

"You look just like my mother," Donny said, smiling.

And, Flippy had to admit, the woman in the picture did look strangely familiar. According to the papers, Gracie had been burned badly in the fire. Flippy had not learned if she had died in the fire or not. Perhaps she was home.

Donny led her into a small room with bunk beds.

"This is Donny's room. I have bunk beds. I can sleep on the bottom or on the top. One night I sleep on the bottom. One night I sleep on the top." There was another picture of Gracie Willis with her two boys.

Then they walked into Rodney's room.

"This is Rodney's room. Rodney takes care of me."

Flippy could sense the dark energy as soon as she crossed the threshold. The bed was made neatly. There was a Bible on the nightstand, and several other things displayed like trophies on a table. Ponytail holders, eyeglasses, a bracelet. Not just any bracelet. It was Traci's bracelet. Flippy had given it to her last year. Flippy picked up the bracelet.

"Who does this belong to?"

"That belongs to my girlfriend. Rodney has a lot of girlfriends."

Flippy put the bracelet in her pants pocket.

"Are there any other rooms?"

"The auditorium."

"You have an auditorium in the house?"

"It's in the back of the house. Rodney built it. Sometimes he lets me watch, if I'm good. That's where he brings his girlfriends."

Flippy's stomach lurched. She'd already sensed she'd made a mistake by coming here. She had stumbled onto a House of Horrors, the home of a monstrous serial killer. She was sure of it. And she needed to get out of here as fast as she could, make it back to the bus before the killer came home.

"Show me the auditorium, and then I really have to go."

Donny went to a drawer in the living room and got a key. They walked down a long, dark hallway, and he used the key to open the auditorium door.

Flippy couldn't believe what she was seeing. It was a duplicate in miniature of the Performing Arts Center auditorium where the homecoming pageant took place, complete with spotlights, a hardwood floor stage, and a backstage dressing room, even auditorium-style seating. No money had been spent on the front of the house, but this room must have cost a fortune.

"What does Rodney do in the auditorium?"

"This is where he takes his girlfriends when they visit."

"Are there any other rooms I should see?"

"There's Rodney's workshop, but I don't have a key to that. Rodney says that room is off limits."

Off limits. Was that where the killer tortured and burned his victims, in the privacy of his "workshop?" Where no one could hear their screams? Was that where he had killed Traci?

All right, this was her opportunity. Sure, she was scared, and she knew she was stupid for coming here alone, but she was here, so she forged ahead.

"Can we see Rodney's workshop? I want to see your brother's workshop."

"Rodney's workshop is strictly off limits."

"Well, can't you make an exception?"

"Only Rodney's girlfriends can go there. Are you Rodney's girlfriend?"

Flippy was repulsed at that thought, but she answered weakly, "Yes."

"Well, then, I guess it's okay. But he won't be happy. Rodney said his workshop is strictly off limits."

Chapter Twenty-One

Luke ran into the office and shook Misty's shoulders.

"Where is she?" Luke shouted. "Has she shown up yet?"

"Luke, you're hurting me."

Luke was desperate, but he colored as he realized what he had done.

Luke paced the office. "I'm sorry, but I'm worried sick about her. I should never have left her alone. If she's not at DaVinci's and she's not at home, where is she?"

He bounded into her office. Her purse was on her desk, along with the manila file. The file that had been missing since last night. The file Flippy had taken from his condo.

There had to be a clue here as to her whereabouts. He rifled through the file until he came to a circled name. Rodney Willis, maintenance. Then he found the crumpled newspaper article about the fire, the beauty queen mother, and the older brother, and he began to put it together. Holy shit. Flippy had found the killer. The address in the article was the same as the house Kate had described, the one at the end of the bus route. Luke rubbed the back of his neck. He had a terrible feeling. Katherine had been right. The killer was focused on Flippy. Surely Flippy couldn't be stupid enough to have gone there on her own. Without her cell phone. And without contacting him. Or had Rodney Willis kidnapped her from outside her office? Neither of those scenarios made him feel any better.

"Anything else?" Luke snapped.

"This fax just came in from Ajax Production Company, the one Philippa has been waiting for. Ajax is the company that produced the homecoming pageant video. They sent over a list of people who purchased the video and the name of the man who shot it."

Misty stomped back to her desk.

Luke scanned the list and compared it to the list of employee names in his file. The name stood out like a neon sign. Rodney Willis.

"I'm calling it in," Luke said to an empty office, as he picked up the phone and dialed police headquarters to give them the particulars.

"I'm sure," he said over the phone. "I'm goddamn sure. I'll meet you over there. Contact Director Beckham. And get someone over to where Rodney Willis works. I don't know exactly where he is, but find him and find him fast. He's got Philippa Tannenbaum."

He sprinted into the outer office. "I want you to call me if you hear *anything* from her. Pray to God we do hear something from her, and soon."

"I'm sorry, Luke."

Luke relented. "It's not your fault." He bounded outside and walked over to the rosebushes. "Matt, are you in there?" He told Flippy he'd sent someone over to spell him. Matt Bauer, his partner on the force. Matt was supposed to pose as a homeless man and keep an eye out for Flippy, but he was gone, too, and Luke couldn't reach him on his cell phone.

"Shit."

"She took the bus," said a voice from the bushes. "Miss Tannenbaum took the bus."

"Who are you?" Luke grabbed the man by the scruff of his shirt.

"My name's Chuck. I was stretching my legs and I saw her get on the Number 5."

"The Number 5?" Luke pulled out his cell and dialed the office. I need the route for the Number 5 city bus." Then to the homeless man he was still holding he said, "Have you seen any strange people here lately?"

"There's a new man who showed up here yesterday. He got on the bus with Miss Tannenbaum."

Luke breathed again. It was Matt. Matt had followed Flippy. Matt was armed, but why hadn't he called in or answered his phone?

"Are you going to find Miss Tannenbaum?"

"Yes. I hope so."

"I'm coming with you. You could use me."

"Yes, I can use all the help I can get. Thanks. My car's over here." The two got into Luke's car and drove off. Luke was waiting for a call-back to confirm the route, but he knew what the answer would be. 5555 Skyline Road would be on that route, and that bastard Willis had Philippa.

His cell phone rang. It was the call he was expecting, with the answer he was expecting. And he got some more information that made him sick. Rodney Willis had not come to work today. He'd called in sick. He was sick all right, Luke thought. And he had taken the only thing that mattered to Luke. "We don't have much time," he said to Chuck, muttering to himself, "I hope we're not too late."

Chapter Twenty-Two

Flippy was about to enter Rodney's workshop when the spotlights went on. Then a disembodied voice that sounded as smooth as a radio DJ's floated over the loudspeaker. What she heard sent a chill down her spine.

"Philippa Tannenbaum. Step up to the stage. So glad you could join us. We've been waiting for you."

Flippy staggered backwards. She was trapped.

"Were you thinking of leaving us? I wouldn't advise it. We're waaaay out in the woods at the End of the World, and nobody knows you're here. So relax. You'll find your wardrobe in the changing area in back of the stage. I'm sure you're familiar with this room. I built it for you."

Flippy wasn't sure she'd heard correctly.

"Yes, I know what you're thinking. But it's true. I built this room with you in mind. That's right. I saw you in last year's pageant. You should have won the pageant. You are much more beautiful and poised than the bitch who took your title. You're no runner-up. I wanted to tell you myself, but I thought of another way. A way that would get everyone's attention. Then in this year's pageant, when I saw you were the pageant director, I thought of the perfect way to honor you. You know my mother, Gracie Willis, she was Miss Graysville, and then the next year she was up for the county title and someone stole it from her. She was first runner-up. I couldn't help my mother, but I can help you. By eliminating the competition, literally."

Flippy shuddered.

"Where are you?" she called out. Disoriented, she couldn't see the man speaking because he was shielded by the blinding lights.

"That's none of your concern. You know what I'm capable of, so, please—don't waste my time. Go and change into the first outfit I've laid out. In my mother's day, before all this women's lib nonsense, they hadn't banned bikinis from the pageant. I know they don't do this anymore, but it's my pageant. I love a good bathing suit competition. Don't you? All that beautiful, smooth, bare skin."

Flippy tried to run for the door when she heard a shot ring out and saw the wood next to her head splinter. She ducked.

"You don't want to do that, Philippa—or should I call you Flippy? I think I'll call you Flippy. It's so much more personal. And we're going to get to know each other very well before this week is over."

"Donny, take a seat. You're going to love this show. All the others were just preludes. I was just warming up."

Flippy walked up the steps on the left side of the stage and walked into the dressing area. She saw three outfits laid out, marked "#1," "#2," and "#3." The first was a skimpy bikini, the second was casual wear, and the third was the evening gown.

Shaking, Flippy undressed behind the curtain and put on the bikini. What choice did she have? If she could keep him talking, she could stay alive. She could get answers to her questions, and maybe somebody would figure out she was here. But nobody knew she was here. Nobody would put it together. She knew this was the end. She was going to die here, just like the other girls. Just like Traci. She reached into the pocket of the skirt she'd been wearing, fished out Jack's ring, and put it on her right hand. If she didn't survive this ordeal, and they found her body, she wanted Jack to have his ring back. Then she lifted Traci's bracelet from her pocket and fastened it around her left wrist—the last keepsake of her best friend.

"And now we have Miss Philippa Tannenbaum, looking saucy in her very sexy two-piece. Flippy, front and center. Come out on stage and strut your stuff."

Flippy walked hesitantly onto the stage.

"Model the suit for us. You know the drill. My, my, who knew what was under all those layers."

Flippy's body shook uncontrollably. Not just from the cold. The auditorium was ice cold, but fright had taken hold of her barely-clad body.

"Now, now. I can see you're shy. Just a case of stage fright. My mother was shy, too. Or at least I thought she was. She hid it well behind miles of eyelashes, when all along my mother was nothing but a tramp."

Flippy shuddered. This man was seriously disturbed.

"All right, now, Donny. You can take the picture now. Usually I do the makeup first, but you don't need makeup. I wouldn't change a thing about that fabulous face of yours. That's right, Donny. A nice close-up on Miss Tannenbaum's best assets."

A flash went off and blinded Flippy. She almost

tripped in the high heels Rodney had supplied for the outfit.

"Lovely. Lovely. All right now, hurry, hurry, and go change into your casual wear outfit. The black leather bustier with the black silk taffeta skirt. And don't forget the black leather gloves. They'll round out the outfit quite nicely."

Flippy teetered back to the changing area, put on the second outfit, and stepped out onto the stage.

"Splendid. Now show us what you've got. That's right. Work it. Donny, did you get that? Did you capture the moment? I picked out those outfits myself."

Flippy walked the runway, first hesitantly, then more confidently. She wasn't going to let this bastard get the better of her. When the time was right, she'd strike back. She wasn't going to end up like Traci.

"Now you're getting the hang of it."

Flippy faced her adversary. "Why don't you show your face, you bastard. You killed my best friend."

"Actually, Traci Farris was just collateral damage. I was there that night for you. That little twit just got in the way. I've been watching you for a long time. That girl stole your man. What do you care about her? I killed her for you, saved you the trouble."

Flippy choked. "You're sick."

"She was nothing but a little whore, just like my mother. Okay, now for the evening gown competition."

"Rodney, did you hurt Traci? I thought you said she'd gone home."

"Don't listen to anything she says, Donny. Women can't be trusted. How many times have I told you that? They turn everything around to deceive and confuse us. Remember the story about Adam and Eve and the

Original Sin, from the Bible?"

Donny nodded.

While Rodney spewed his hatred of women, Flippy went to the changing room. The gown was gorgeous. It was a pure white silk, seeded with pearls, almost like a wedding gown. It was a vintage gown, and it was a perfect fit. She came out of the dressing room.

"Brava. You look magnificent in that gown. Just like my mother did. That was her gown. The gown she wore when she won Miss Graysville."

"Why are you killing all those girls?" Flippy demanded.

"Oh, that's all going to stop, now that I have you. I've saved the best for last. You'll be my best work of art. Now, model for all you're worth. Model as if your life depends on it, because it does."

Flippy walked up and down the stage several times until she heard the voice.

"Donny, let's capture this for posterity. Beautiful. This will make a nice addition to the photo gallery. And be sure the video camera is rolling. Philippa, I can't wait for you to see my photo gallery and my new video. It's right in the next room. You haven't seen my workroom, but that's our next stop. It's where I do my finest work. And I have just the final resting place for you. It's one you never even thought of. You and that new man of yours. Yes, I've been watching you. I know all about Officer Luke Slaughter."

Flippy raised her head, but she still couldn't distinguish the face of the speaker.

"You'd better not hurt Luke."

"Oh, I will, but not physically. But when he sees what will happen to you, he'll be devastated." Then

Rodney Willis began to laugh and his voice resonated around the room.

Flippy was shaking.

"All right, you can keep the gown on, and go ahead, grab a stole from the dressing room. I know I keep it cold in here, but it's better for my burns. That's right, you can't see my face. If you did, you might be frightened. And I don't want you to be frightened, yet. When I decide to show myself, we'll be all up close and personal, and we'll have plenty of face time."

Flippy blanched as she went backstage to retrieve the stole.

"Perfect. Now for the question-and-answer session. Are you ready? Here's the first question."

Flippy heard some feedback from the microphone.

"Donny, would you please adjust the mike?"

Donny ambled over to the control room.

"Why are women such whores?" Rodney called out.

Flippy stood still.

"Come on, you know the answer to that question. You had a boyfriend for four years, you were engaged, and yet that very night you went out and slept with another man. Don't bother to deny it. As I said, I've been watching you. Do you have the answer to my question? And I'll know if it's not the truth."

"I was angry at Jack for cheating on me. I was drunk."

"Then how do you explain sleeping with Luke again?"

Flippy was quiet as she considered her answer. Somehow the man must have been spying on them in Luke's condo, or else how could he possibly know that?

"I-I love him." And she knew it was true but she'd never get a chance to tell him.

"Ah, love. I know how that feels. Only it's all one-sided. I love you, do you know that, Philippa? But if you saw me you wouldn't give me the time of day. My mother said she loved me. But how did she show it? When I came home from school, I found her in bed with another man. Naked, bodies tangled, doing the dirty deed right in front of me. Of course she jumped up when she saw me, and apologized, but it was too late. The whore had to be punished."

"So you set your house on fire purposely?"

"Donny, you can leave the room now. Go develop those pictures just like I taught you. I want to be alone with Miss Tannenbaum."

Donny left the room obediently.

"Did he have anything to do with these murders?"

"Do you see him? He's as innocent as a babe. He has no idea what's really going on. I've got to protect him. He does help, unintentionally. Lures in the girls, but he's never been in my workshop. It's a bit messy in there. I'm afraid he'd slip on all the blood. Of course my older brother is big and strong, and he helps me carry my special sacks to the drop-off points. He doesn't know what's in them."

"So did you murder your mother?"

"Murder is such a nasty word. I did light her bedroom on fire and lock the door and step outside so I wouldn't hear her screams. Then I relented and opened the door, and when I saw my mother's beautiful face burning, I put out the fire. I saved my mother. But unfortunately, I was burned in the process. But she paid for her sins. She had to live with her ugly face and her shame until the day she couldn't live with it anymore. She couldn't work, couldn't show her face, couldn't get a man. So she took my stepfather's shotgun and shot herself. Blew off her face. I buried her out back. But I miss her. She was the most beautiful woman I've ever seen, until I saw you. You look just like her, you know. That's why I chose you. Had to have you."

"Why did you have to kill Traci and the other girls?"

"Now, I'm asking the questions here. But I'll answer this one last question. Why did I kill the girls? I loved their beauty, their perfection, I reveled in it, but then they had to be punished."

"So you burned the sides of their faces while they were still alive?"

"Yes, recreating the past. I marked them. I let them think I was going to save them at the last minute, but alas, they couldn't be saved. You'll see exactly how it happens. Come now, I'm ready to reveal myself."

Rodney Willis stepped into view. His face was hideous, all scarred and puffy.

Flippy cringed.

He strode up to her and she turned to run.

"I still have bullets in this gun, so you won't get far." She froze.

Rodney grabbed her and twisted her arms behind her back and tied them. He dragged her along the walkway and unlocked another room.

Flippy almost fainted at the sight of it. It was like a medieval torture room. Photos of Traci and the other victims were posted all around the walls. She spotted the body of another one of the contestants, Dana Lyons. Was she dead or merely asleep? Rodney approached

Flippy and tried to smother her with a white handkerchief. The room was spinning and then everything went black.

When she came to, she was tied to a table, still dressed in the gown and heels she'd worn in the "pageant," and staring into the disfigured face of her killer.

"Why are you doing this to me?" she cried, straining against her bonds.

"I already told you. Because it gives me pleasure. And I have so little of that in my life. But you'll be my last. You can take comfort in that. Usually, I let the girls linger for the better part of a week, starve them, deprive them of water until they're weak and vulnerable, and then I go to work on them. Burn their faces while they're still alive, and show them a mirror so they can see what's left of their former beauty. A little torture, but not enough that they can't take it, and then, mercifully, I put them out of their misery before I go to work."

Flippy struggled on the table.

"It's all documented on the videotape." Rodney flicked a switch and the lights went out. Images of Rodney with his victims appeared on a large screen. Bound, she had no choice but to watch it, the way he'd captured each of his victims, bound them, burned them, their last walk down the runway, the torture on his workroom table, and the bodies deposited at the dump sites. The footage of Traci was the hardest to watch.

"And I am most sorry about you," Rodney lamented. "Because I do love you, you know. In fact, I worship you. I would do anything for you. But would you love me back? Could you?"

Flippy felt the bile rise in her stomach. Then she spit in his face.

"Feisty. I like that. You know I don't take sexual liberties with my women. Not that I don't want to, but I can't. That ability was taken away in the fire. But I get my satisfaction in other ways."

Flippy sagged. The full realization that no one was coming to rescue her made her sad. She'd miss Luke the most. She'd never see his face again, and now that she knew she loved him, she wouldn't have the chance to tell him. And that was real torture.

Rodney freed one of her hands and placed something in it.

"Okay, you can hold the mirror, Queenie's mirror."

Rodney struck a match and held the flame to her face, bringing it closer and closer, till it was only inches away.

"What a shame the flame will mar such beauty." She could feel the heat, and she shrank away and then he touched the fire to her face and she cried out.

"It will only hurt for a minute. Once I've marked you as mine, no one else will want you. No one else will be able to stand looking at you. Not Jack, and I see you're still wearing his ring. Foolish girl. And not Officer Luke. And then, once you realize I'm all you have left, we can be together and we will be happy."

"Flippy, are you in there?"

"Luke!" she cried, trying to turn toward his voice. "Over here!" Luke rushed to her side as Rodney looked up and laughed. He held out the flame and with his other hand drew his gun, but Luke was faster. He knocked the flame out of Rodney's hand and they struggled for the gun. The flame lit the rug on fire and started to spread, licking the drapes and igniting the wooden furniture. Then Luke had the gun, but Rodney escaped the room like a rabbit.

Luke untied Flippy and set her upright, touching her hair, and her face, trying to convince himself she was really there in front of him.

"Are you okay? I was scared to death when I couldn't find you."

"I'm fine, but you got here just in time. Rodney Willis is the killer. I can prove it. Look around. He has the photos of all the dead girls. And he has a video. It's all there, all the murders, the torture, all on a video. Get it, Luke."

"We don't have time for that—this place is about to go up."

"Get Dana. She's one of the missing girls. She's over there on the floor in the corner."

"Flip, we don't have another second to spare."

From the corner of her eye, she saw Chuck, the homeless man, running toward the motionless girl.

"I'll get the other girl. You take care of Miss Tannenbaum," Chuck said.

"But your evidence, it's all here." The pictures of the contestants were curling into ash, melting in the intense heat.

"You're the only thing I care about. The police are on their way. That freakshow bushwhacker shot my partner Matt and left him to bleed out in the field down the road. The paramedics said he was going to be okay. Matt was coming after you. He was riding on the bus."

"How did you know where to find me?"

"Kate called me and said you were in trouble. But we can talk about that later. Let's get out of here."

They fled the burning room, and when they got outside, Dana was lying on the grass, choking, but the paramedics had revived her. Chuck was holding Rodney.

"What is Chuck doing here?"

"I deputized your homeless friend. I'll explain later." Luke grabbed Rodney by the throat.

"You're going down, dickhead."

There were screams from the house.

"My brother Donny is in there," Rodney said, and before Luke could cuff him he broke away from Luke's grip and ran into the flames.

Flippy heard police and fire truck sirens approaching, but the wooden house had gone up like a matchstick. It was too late to save it. There were more screams, and Rodney came running through the flames with his brother wrapped in a sheet dripping with cold water. He carried his brother to safety, but Rodney himself was on fire, and Flippy would never forget the piteous screams that came out of him. Police raced to get to him, but they were too late. Finally, he was quiet, and there was only a burning hulk where there had once been a man.

Luke handled her as if she were breakable. He checked and rechecked her as police sirens and ambulances signaled their approach.

"Are you sure you're okay?"

"Really, I'm fine," Flippy assured Luke, leaning up against him.

The police had Donny and Dana on stretchers, and the EMTs were treating them for smoke inhalation.

"What will happen to Donny? I don't think he knew what was going on in that pageant of horrors. I think his brother was the mastermind."

"I don't know, Flip. If that's true and there were extenuating circumstances, then maybe—"

"But he has no one now."

"What did I say about that bleeding heart of yours? Now let's get you home where you belong," Luke said, wrapping his arm around Flippy.

"Where is home?"

"With me, of course," Luke said, flashing a smile and dimples that weakened her willpower and plunged her deeper in love with the man.

"Dudley Do-Right to the rescue?" She smiled.

"Every story has a happy ending."

"We have to make one stop before we get home," Flippy said.

"Where to?"

Flippy touched the ring on her hand and looked at Luke.

"To return this."

"You're wearing Jack's ring again?" Luke frowned and his dimples disappeared.

"I took it with me so I could give it back."

The dimples were back in full bloom. "And I'm going to replace it as soon as possible with my ring. How do you feel about that?"

"Sounds perfect," Flippy said.

A cloud of dust signaled the arrival of another patrol car. Jack, Katherine, Chief Bradley, and Flippy's director rushed out of the squad car and crowded around her.

"Sorry we're late to the party," said Chief Bradley, wrapping Philippa in a bear hug. Are you okay?" Flippy blushed.

"I'm fine, Chief Bradley."

"Philippa, what possessed you to come out here all alone?" yelled Director Beckham. "I thought we had an arrangement. You were going to call me before you took any action." The director was stern-faced, and then she did something totally out of character. She hugged Flippy and kissed her forehead.

"You scared me half to death, Philippa."

"I had to be sure, Director, before I notified you."

Kate hugged her next. "I was so frightened. I was afraid you weren't going to make it out alive."

"You don't know how close I came to death. If Luke hadn't come along when he did, I wouldn't be here."

"I owe a lot to Kate," Luke admitted. "She was a big help. Plus, you left a trail a mile wide in the folder on your desk and with the imprint of this address on the notepad in your office."

The chief patted Luke on the back. "Great work, son. I'm going to see that you get that promotion to detective. And Philippa, you solved the case, with a little help from Crystal Ball Kate. After you've had a chance to recover, I want you to be the one to make the announcement that we've solved the case of the Homecoming Homicides. And if I'm not mistaken, Elizabeth, it's going to mean Philippa also gets a substantial raise in salary and position. That's a number one performance you delivered."

Flippy smiled and squeezed Luke's hand.

Kate, apparently relieved that the whole ordeal was over, took the chief aside. "Chief Bradley, do you ever get up to Atlanta? There's someone I'd like you to meet."

"Is she hot?"

The director rolled her eyes.

"She's smokin'," Jack assured the chief, as he watched the remains of the dilapidated house of horrors burn to the ground. "Looks exactly like my wife."

"I think we ought to introduce Chief Bradley to my mother—I mean, to Juliette. They'd make a nice couple. I think they could have a future together."

"If you have a thing for psychics, then you'll love Kate's mom," Jack agreed. "That woman is eerie-scary the way she can predict the future."

"Can't wait to meet her," Chief Bradley said. "Let's set this up sooner rather than later."

"I think I can accommodate you. I've got a proposition I want to discuss with you back at the office," Jack said.

"Great. But right now I've got me a serial killer case to put to bed." He looked at the charred body in the grass. "That the guy?"

"That's the killer," Flippy confirmed. "Or was. His brother is the one in the ambulance. You're going to want to question him as an accessory or a witness. I'm not sure which. And there's the last missing girl, Dana Lyons, in the second ambulance. She's traumatized, but alive, and Chuck, here, is responsible for carrying her out."

The chief turned to Chuck.

"I'm grateful to you. I could use a man like you on the force. Are you available?"

Chuck beamed. "I'm about to start a new job, but I'd love to talk to you about another opportunity."

"Luke, you bring Philippa down to the station, and we'll get her statement, find out what went on in that house, and then you can take her home."

He turned his attention to the director.

"Elizabeth, I'll drive you back to the station so we can sort this out. Jack and Katherine, will I see you back at the station?"

"We'll be there," Jack promised, wrapping Kate in his arms and joining Luke and Philippa.

Chief Bradley and the director walked toward the squad car, head to head, parsing the details of the case.

"That Chief Bradley is not bad to look at." Flippy giggled. "Not that I'm looking."

"And he's horny as a hound dog," Luke added.

"Maybe that's just what Juliette needs," Jack said.

Luke turned to Flippy, touched his forehead to hers and whispered, "And you are just what I need."

Chapter Twenty-Three

As Luke and Flippy walked hand and hand down the grassy path to Luke's car, Jack caught his wife's eye and nodded to Kate.

"Looks like our work is done here, babe. Let's stop by the station, square things with Chief Bradley, get our things from the hotel, and head home to our own Romeo and Juliette."

"I can't wait to get back home."

Jack coughed. "Uh, honey, about that. I've got a surprise for you."

Kate looked doubtful. "Does this surprise have to do with serial killers?"

"No," Jack said, "but it does have to do with a possible murder."

"Oh, Jack, we're newlyweds. Barely back from our honeymoon in Bermuda. Can't we take a break from murder?"

"I think you're going to like this new assignment."

Kate sighed. "Apparently your mind is already made up. Why don't you tell me about it?"

"Juliette got a call from the Atlantis Cruise Company. They've been getting threatening emails. Their newest ship is scheduled for a repositioning cruise from Barcelona to Miami this weekend, and someone has threatened to do harm to the ship and its passengers. The captain and crew are very superstitious and refuse to board the ship unless they have protection or assurances that someone is handling this matter."

"What's a repositioning cruise?" Kate asked.

"Cruise ships need to be in warm water during the colder months of the year, so cruise lines move their European ships to the Caribbean during the fall and back to Europe in the spring," explained Jack. "But they don't want to sail with an empty ship so they offer passengers repositioning cruises when they move the ships in the spring and fall. Repositioning cruises are typically longer than normal cruises without as many ports of call, which means more days at sea, more onboard amenities and tremendous cost savings from high season rates."

"I still think the local police would be better equipped to handle this case."

"The ship's registry is the Marshall Islands," Jack said. "The cruise starts out in Barcelona, but then it goes out to sea and makes several island stopovers, so there's an issue of jurisdiction. And, they specifically asked for Crystal Ball Kate."

"How did they even hear about me?"

"You're world famous, Kate."

"I still think the police could do a better job," Kate insisted.

"According to our new client, the matter involves some sensitivity, as well as some urgency, as the passengers are scheduled to embark this Sunday."

"And talk about barking, what about Romeo? Where will she go?"

"Mama has agreed to babysit Romeo."

"Looks like you've thought of everything. But a murder hasn't even been committed yet. What if this is a hoax, a way to extort money from the cruise line?"

"The cruise line fears for the safety of its passengers, the crew, and their own reputation. They can't afford to take any chances with lives or livelihood. Passengers are fickle. One sinking, one fire, one passenger gone overboard or murdered aboard ship, and, just like that"—he snapped his fingers—"bookings dry up."

"What did you mean by sensitivity?"

"Apparently there are portents of a psychic nature plaguing that ship."

"Portents?"

"Strange crew sightings. One of the crew spotted three gulls flying toward him, always a bad omen."

"Some people think a woman aboard ship brings bad luck," said Kate. "Next thing you'll be telling me is that one of the crew thought he spotted a mermaid. A sure sign of disaster."

"There's much more to this, I assure you. First thing we have to do is interview the crew and try to figure out who the victim or victims might possibly be."

"Jack, why can't we just go home and rest? This has been a rough week for me, and I know it has for you."

"Kate, just imagine—fun, sun, and sex on the high seas. You've been telling me you want to relax. If we take this assignment, we get a free cruise. Free airfare to Barcelona and then back home from Miami. Luxurious accommodations—a suite on the concierge floor with our own private veranda. Spas, heated pools. Gourmet food. Entertainment. It's first class all the way. We'll be posing as honeymooners, so we won't even have to pretend. Think of it, Kate, a twelve-day trip on a midsize luxury ship, with stops at fascinating ports—Morocco, Portugal, and Bermuda. I've never been on a cruise before, babe."

Kate shook her head. Jack was hard to refuse.

"You sound like a brochure for the cruise line," Kate said. "You said *if* we take this assignment. You've already accepted it, haven't you?"

"I'm really psyched about this. I thought you would be too."

"It sounds lovely, two weeks aboard ship with a killer."

"Kate." Jack slumped, deflated.

"I'll miss Juliette. I'm just getting to know her."

"That's the beauty of it, honey. We're going to take Juliette along. I think we could use someone with her psychic skills to work with you. And I'm going to talk to Chief Bradley about coming with us to work under cover. He has a lot of experience in law enforcement. He can pose as Juliette's husband, just an average couple celebrating their anniversary."

"There's nothing average about Juliette," Kate noted. "Has she agreed to this?"

"Yes. She's never been on a cruise before either. She has all our documents ready. And she's packed for you, plenty of those skimpy bikinis you wore on our honeymoon in Bermuda."

Kate rolled her eyes. "As I recall, you didn't let me wear much of anything during our honeymoon. I never even cut the tags off."

"Exactly. They'll be as good as new."

"When do we leave?"

"We fly out tomorrow night."

"What about Chief Bradley? Is Juliette ready to

share a cabin and a bed with a perfect stranger?"

"I haven't filled her in on that part yet. But that way, they can get a taste of each other, so to speak."

"Trapped in the same cabin for almost two weeks, I guess anything could happen."

"Juliette is lonely, and Chief Bradley needs a woman in his life," Jack reasoned.

"It sounds like you're trying to pimp out my mother—uh, Juliette."

"I just want everyone to be as happy as we are."

"Good save, Beauregard."

Jack breathed a long sigh of relief. "I'm glad that's settled. Bon Voyage!"

Read an excerpt from the third book in the Psychic Crystal Mystery series:

Murder on the Repositioning Cruise

by
Marilyn Baron

A Psychic Crystal Mystery
Book Three

Marilyn Baron

Juliette Spencer stared at the ill-mannered boor leering at her breasts like he was stalking his prey or scoping out his next meal. Like he wanted to inhale her or impale her or worse. Like she was Bambi and it was open season on single women sporting a deer-in-the-headlights demeanor.

How did the rutting buck's horns manage to stay on his swelled head? His buff body filled the stateroom they would be sharing for the next two weeks, and the overpowering odor of the man's aftershave was stifling in such close quarters. This suite wasn't big enough for both of them. And there was no escape, short of jumping off the ship, which she had half a mind to do. She could go out on the balcony and breathe in the night air, but she was trapped—"married" to this bozo for the remainder of the cruise.

She knew exactly what the sheriff was thinking. And it made her blush. Being psychic had its advantages *and* disadvantages. He was thinking he could have her anytime he wanted. All he had to do was flash that becoming smile of his and flex those overdeveloped muscles, barely disguised in his body-hugging T-shirt.

Turning away, she found herself gazing into a mirror, which only made matters worse. Objects in the mirror are closer than they appear, she thought. Well, he could think again. She wasn't going to go all gooey over a green-eyed small-town lawman. This was business, even if the sheriff had plans to combine this assignment with pleasure—*his* pleasure.

He knew about her tainted history in Casa Spirito and her sordid relationship with the Reverend Carter Coulter. The whole world knew about it. It had happened practically in his own backyard. So, of course, he thought he knew her and what she'd be willing to do, for him and to him. And the fact that she could read him like a book didn't leave much to the imagination.

Blowing out a breath, she turned to face him. She'd just have to make do, dismiss the dimples and ignore the abs. This was an opportunity to get to know her daughter better, and after they solved the mystery, spend a relaxing cruise with Kate and her new son-in-law, Jack.

Dangerous and distasteful as he was, the sheriff was part of the package. Andy of Mayberry he was not. Not a redeeming bone in his sculpted body. If she was looking to fall in love again, which she very definitely wasn't, Sheriff Will Bradley was the last man on earth she would give her heart to.

A word about the author...

Marilyn Baron is a PRO member of Romance Writers of America (RWA) and Georgia Romance Writers (GRW) and winner of the GRW 2009 Chapter Service Award and writing awards in single title, suspense, and paranormal romance. A former GRW board member and past editor of the chapter's online newsletter, *The Galley*, she handled Publicity for GRW's 2013 Moonlight & Magnolias Conference. She also belongs to Marketing for Romance Writers. She writes in a variety of genres, from humorous women's fiction to romantic suspense/thrillers, historicals and paranormal.

Born in Miami, Florida, Marilyn graduated from the University of Florida in Gainesville and now lives in Roswell, Georgia, with her husband.

Marilyn says: What's unique about my writing? I try to inject humor into everything I write. I like to laugh and my readers do too. I tend to feature older heroines, because, let's face it, we're not getting any younger. I love to travel. My favorite place to visit is Italy, but I also love Bermuda. I think readers will love "visiting" this romantic and exotic destination getaway in *UNDER THE MOON GATE* and its prequel *DESTINY: A BERMUDA LOVE STORY*, and find it as charming and inviting as I do.

To find out more about Marilyn's books, please visit her Web site at:

www.marilynbaron.com

and her blog, Petit Fours and Hot Tamales at:

http://www.petitfoursandhottamales.com/